# All the Right Reasons

## A Grady Romance: Book 2

# Stephanie Renee

# Prologue

JESSIE

*leven years ago...*

"What are you thinking about?" I look over at my best friend, Tracy, leaning back in her chair, letting the sunlight hit her face.

She sighs but doesn't open her eyes. "I'm thinking about how all of your talking is going to scare the fish away."

My knee bobs up and down anxiously while I hold onto my fishing pole in my left hand. "I'm bored," I grumble in a quieter tone than before.

"Can you just relax and enjoy the beautiful day? The sun's shining, and the birds are chirping. I'd say that makes it pretty perfect out here."

"But the damn fish aren't biting," I reply, annoyed.

"Because they hear your big mouth. All your negative energy is making them run for the hills."

"Don't you mean *swim* for the hills?" I laugh at my horrible attempt at a joke, but Tracy just rolls her eyes.

When we fall silent again, I shift in my chair, unable to sit still.

Tracy finally sits up and looks over at me. "Are you okay? You usually love fishing."

When I don't respond, she goes on, "Does this have anything to do with the fact that your daddy is back in town?"

I still don't say a word, but my answer is clear when my eyes avoid hers.

"Do you want to talk about it?" She asks.

"Not even a little bit," I mumble.

"Okay, you don't want to be quiet, but you don't want to talk about anything serious. So what *do* you want to talk about, Mr. Chatty?"

My shoulders shrug, and she sighs. I know she's getting annoyed with me.

"Do you want to talk about how Abigail Cheney practically threw herself at you at the school dance the other night?" She asks like it's no big deal, but I swear I hear a hint of jealousy in her tone.

Tracy and I never put much stock into school dances. We never go with dates, only with each other. And usually, we just go to goof on them most of the time.

She's right, though. The other night, Abigail was trying a little too hard to get my attention. But truth be told, no matter how hard Abigail tried, Tracy was the only one I was looking at.

She's the only one I'm always looking at. But she has absolutely no idea of that fact.

I realize I've been quiet for a minute now, and she's staring at me. Joking, while still trying to put her mind at ease, I say, "Oh, come on, T. You know you're the only girl for me."

She scoffs. "You're so full of shit."

"One of these days, T, you'll see the light. One day, I'm going to marry you."

She laughs. "Oh? Do I get a say in this?"

"Well, duh. But see, I have a plan."

She readjusts in her seat, getting comfortable. "Oh, I can't wait to hear this."

"Do you remember that promise we made a few years ago?" I ask.

"Which one? We are always making each other promises."

"True. But this one was special. You and I promised each other that if we weren't married by the time we turn forty, we

2

would marry each other."

She shrugs. "So what?"

I smile. "So, I'll hold you to that promise."

Her laugh echoes off the lake. "How can you be so sure that I'll still be single when I'm forty? Am I really that repulsive to men?"

"Not at all. I think you'll have men falling all over you."

"But I won't be married?" She looks at me like I'm completely full of shit.

"Nope. Because you, Tracy Kennedy, know how special you are, and you aren't going to settle for some jerk who doesn't treat you right."

"And you think you're going to break the mold? You're going to be the one I fall madly in love with and want to marry?"

I snap my fingers and point at her. "You got it. And I am pretty confident it will happen long before we are forty."

She purses her lips together. "Your cockiness amazes me."

Tracy Kennedy and I have never even kissed before, but there's no doubt in my mind that she's the girl I want to grow old with.

We may just be kids, but I know a good thing when I see one. We both have a whole lot of living to do, but I know no matter what, we'll always find our way back to each other.

Because that's what soulmates do.

And whether or not she knows it, that's what Tracy and I are—soulmates.

One day, I'll show her just how good we'd be together. We made a promise to marry each other when we're older. I intend to keep it and just hope and pray it happens long before we're forty.

# Chapter One

## TRACY

"So, you own your own business?" The man sitting across the table asks. His name is Todd, and we are on an extremely awkward blind date.

I nod in response to his question. "Yeah, it's a small boutique in my hometown of Grady. We sell clothes and accessories for women and teens."

Before I can say anything else on the subject, Todd begins speaking again. "That must keep you pretty busy. Do you plan on selling the business when you settle down, get married, and have kids? I can't imagine many men would be okay with you working all the time and not keeping up on the house."

*Oh, Todd is one of THOSE guys.*

Gritting my teeth, I answer, "Well, considering I have no plans of either of those things any time soon, I guess I don't have to worry about that."

My words drip sarcasm, but Todd doesn't seem to pick up on it. Instead, he chuckles. "I guess you're still young and have some time to 'have some fun.'" He puts the words in air quotes. "Personally, I'm at the age where I'm ready to start the next stage. I'd like to find a good woman who will make a good wife."

*No, Todd. It sounds like you want someone who will obey you. Sorry bud, I'll NEVER be that girl.*

He speaks again, "Maybe when you get to be my age, your

priorities will be different. But, eventually, running a business and coming home to an empty bed will get lonely."

"Didn't you say *you* run a business?" I ask.

He narrows his eyes at me. "Yes. But I'm a man. That's what we are supposed to do, darlin'."

My knee bobs frantically up and down in annoyance at his condescending attitude. Finally, I respond with a snarky, "Any man that I consider marrying will love that I'm a business owner and will never encourage me to give it up." I'm not sure such a man exists, but I'm determined to prove Todd wrong.

He gives a slight scoff. One of my employees, Jamie, set this date up, and I have no idea why. This man is a good fifteen years older than me, not to mention a complete and total douche bag. I get that I've been single for a while, but I'm okay with that. I'd rather be single than date assholes like Todd.

I'm grateful as hell when our food arrives. The sooner we can get this date over with, the better.

When Todd texted me to set this up, he asked what kind of food was my favorite. Apparently, he didn't like my answer of Mexican because we are at a fancy French restaurant that I feel utterly underdressed for. So I ordered some pasta because it was the only thing that sounded remotely familiar.

As I dig in, Todd looks at me with a look of mild disgust. "Wow, I'm surprised you're still hungry after all the bread you just ate. You really can eat, huh?"

"I guess. I'm not one of those women who will pick at a salad the whole time."

"Aren't you worried you might get fat?"

*And Todd just keeps getting worse.*

"Well, Todd, I've always had a pretty high metabolism, and I'm fairly active, so I'm not really worried about it. But thank you for your concern for my health."

Again, my sarcasm is lost on my date. Todd goes back to talking about himself. He tells me about the ad agency he owns. He brags about his new, luxurious home but tells me he can't take me there since it's being remodeled.

*Sure it is, Todd.*

After a while, I begin to tune him out as he continues to drone on. Instead, I stare at the way the light shines off of his greasy hair. It's almost blinding.

Then, my attention focuses on the green thing stuck between his yellow teeth. Maybe Todd was good-looking at some point, but now, he looks like that creepy uncle at the Christmas party who tries to sell everyone shitty used cars.

Finally, the waitress drops off our check. She's a young girl who I doubt is even out of high school, but that doesn't stop Todd from staring at her ass as she walks away.

My eyes roll so hard it physically hurts.

He then balks at the check as though he didn't realize a fancy French restaurant would be expensive. He keeps glaring at the bill and then back at me to give me a dirty look.

*Don't look at me, buddy. I would have been good with a couple of cheap tacos.*

He looks like he wants to ask me to pay for my half. At this point, I'd do anything just to make this hell end.

After waging an internal war with himself, he reluctantly puts his credit card in the check holder and sets it all on the table. The waitress quickly takes it to run the card, and we exchange a quick glance. The look in her eyes says she can tell *exactly* how this date is going.

When she brings it back, Todd picks up the slip to sign it, and I see he only left her three dollars on a check that's nearing $100.

"That's all you're going to leave?" I ask.

He shrugs and gives a sleazy smile. "That girl doesn't even look like she's old enough to drive. I guarantee you she doesn't need the money. Besides, if she doesn't like depending on tips, she might want to find a new job."

*The nerve of this guy!*

I know what it's like to wait tables, and let's just say I was no good at it. This girl, on the other hand, has been nothing but fantastic. So she doesn't deserve a crappy $3 tip.

We stand up to leave, and I walk over to the girl and hand her a couple of twenties that I pull from my wallet.

"Not all people are assholes." I wink. She looks as though she might cry at the gesture.

Todd gives me a dirty look as I breeze right past him and out the door. He follows me to my car, and I thank him for dinner.

*He may be an asshole, but I was still raised with those Tennessee manners.*

"The night doesn't have to end here," he says with unmistakable innuendo in his tone.

*I'm surprised this guy can still walk with the giant balls he's toting around.*

"Look, Todd, I think you and I can both agree that this date didn't exactly bring on the fireworks. We have nothing in common, and after this, we'll probably never see each other again."

He sets his hand on my shoulder. "That doesn't mean we can't have some fun tonight."

I remove his arm and wrinkle my forehead. "That's *exactly* what it means."

"Honey, I just spent $100 on dinner. I think you owe me a little something. If you don't want to screw, I'll settle for a blow job."

Thinking this guy *must* be joking, I let out a loud cackle.

But when he forcefully grabs my arm as I try to walk away, I realize that he's nothing but serious.

I try to pull away, but his grip tightens. His longer-than-normal fingernails dig into my skin as he tries to pull me toward his car.

Without another thought, anger overtakes me, and I pull my fist back before lunging forward and making contact with his face.

His hand releases my arm and immediately goes to his nose, which is now gushing blood.

"Bitch! You broke my nose!" He cries.

My Southern accent comes out even thicker than usual.

"Guess you should've kept your hands to yourself, huh?"

Leaving Todd to tend to his bleeding nose, I get in my Jeep and take off.

Rage washes over me at the damn nerve of that asshole. Seriously, who acts like that? And why the fuck would Jamie set me up with him? Do I seem *that* desperate?

Still fuming, I click the call button on my steering wheel and say Jamie's name aloud. Seconds later, the phone is ringing. It takes three rings for Jamie to pick up.

"Hey, Tracy."

"Don't you, 'hey, Tracy,' me. What the fuck were you thinking setting me up with that asshole?"

"Oh..." she stammers.

"Yeah. 'Oh.' Why would you think that I would like that guy? Do you think that my vagina is so desperate for entry that I would let a guy like that into it? Have I pissed you off in some way that I am unaware of? Have I-"

She cuts me off. "Whoa, Trace, calm down. I wasn't trying to sic this dude on you. I promise. I have a little bit of a confession."

"What's that?"

"Honestly, I had no idea who this guy was. My mom set up the date. It was supposed to be for me, but you know I'm dating JD, and..."

Now, I interrupt, "And you don't want your mom to know that you're dating a guy covered in tattoos and piercings."

"Bingo. I figured you were single, and maybe you'd hit it off. My momma had nothing but good things to say about him."

"Your mother is a masochist," I reply sarcastically.

"Maybe a little," she giggles. "So, he was that bad, huh?"

"Jamie, the date ended with me punching him in the face."

"Whoa! What happened?"

I let out a loud groan. "I really just don't have the energy to talk about it anymore tonight. I'll tell you about it next time I see you."

"Okay," she says, sounding almost disappointed.

*Get over it. You set me up with a fucking creep.*

She then asks, "Are you going home for the night?"

"Yeah, I seriously need a beer right now. Shit!" I interrupt my own thoughts. "I'm out of beer."

I look at the clock on my dash and see that the Stop 'N Go, the only market in Grady, is already closed. Damn these small towns.

"Well, I'd invite you over for a cold one," Jamie begins. "But I'm out too."

"It's alright."

"You could always stop into The Saddle."

The Saddle is the only bar in Grady.

"Yeah, maybe," I say. We talk for a moment more before I wrap up the conversation and hang up the phone.

She's got a point. I could go to The Saddle, but I typically try to avoid it. Although I've been a couple of times with friends, I don't ever go alone.

There's a reason for that.

Let's just say I'm actively avoiding my past. I have no idea why, though. It was a lifetime ago.

Deciding that a beer outweighs my emotional bullshit, I turn my car right toward the bar...and the memories I never planned on revisiting.

# Chapter Two

## JESSIE

"**H**ey stud, can I get another drink?"

I look up into the eyes of one of the middle-aged women sitting at the bar here at The Saddle. It's karaoke night, and I'm in hell. Typically, this woman would glare at me if I was walking down the street. But you put a drink in one hand and a microphone in the other, and she stares at me like I'm a piece of meat she's ready to devour.

Quickly, I mix up the dirty martini she ordered. Apparently, karaoke makes her also want to drink fancy martinis instead of the dollar beers she drinks every other night that she's in here.

"Keep the change," she says, handing me some cash.

*Oh boy, a dollar.*

Making my way to the other end of the bar, I lock eyes with a good-looking blonde. She has big brown eyes and blonde hair that hangs in thick curls. Her lips are full and pouty, and her enormous tits are barely contained in the tight dress she's wearing. Based on her tiny frame, I'm guessing they're fake. I prefer real ones, no matter the size, but at the end of the day, tits are tits. Besides, I'm more of an ass and hips man anyway.

I walk over to her, and she orders a vodka and soda. While I make it, she tells me she's just passing through and is looking for a good time. I resist the urge to say to her that I'm not much of a good time these days. I also don't mention that I don't buy her story. No one just 'passes through' Grady. It's barely big enough to be a map dot and isn't close enough to any major highway to be a stop-off.

But I don't care. Everyone has their secrets, and she can keep hers.

We make a little small-talk, and she tells me her name is Courtney. Every time I get a little downtime, I spend it flirting with her.

When she licks that pouty bottom lip of hers and asks if I have a break coming up any time soon, I tell her I'll meet her out back in five minutes.

It might sound sort of jerky of me, but she doesn't seem to mind. And it's been a hell of a long time since my dick has seen any action that wasn't by my own hand.

I finish up what I'm doing and ask one of the waitresses to cover me for a few minutes so that I can take my break.

Once I walk through the back door of the bar, I see Courtney standing in front of my truck with a wicked grin on her face. A grin that shows she wants to get into some trouble.

"Hey, you," she purrs.

Before I can even get my own greeting out, her mouth is on mine. Her tongue delves into my mouth like it's on a mission. Her hand grabs my member through the denim of my jeans, and she starts working me up and down.

The woman is aggressive. That's for sure. And if she keeps it up, I'm going to blow before we even get started. Since I don't like leaving any woman I'm with feeling unsatisfied, I grab her hand.

"Slow down. We've got some time," I whisper.

She gives me another smile, and I lift her, so she's sitting on the hood of my truck. I trail kisses from her jawline down to her neck, and she softly moans. It's sexy, but it almost sounds like she's trying too hard.

I take her face in my hands and kiss her once more. This time, it's a bit more sensual.

When we finally break for air, she pulls back and smiles. Then, she reaches into her bra with her right hand and pulls out a tiny clear bag filled with white powder.

"You want to have some fun?" She asks.

I've done enough cocaine in my life to know what it looks like. I've also done enough of it to know to stay the fuck away from it.

"No thanks," I reply. "I'm good. Maybe this whole thing isn't such a good idea."

Her smile falls at my sudden change of heart.

I add, "I have to get back to work anyway."

Before I can even get through the door, she says, "I heard you were quite the party boy."

"You heard wrong," I growl.

Before heading back to the bar, I stop at the restroom. Trying to calm myself down, I splash some water on my face. It doesn't do much to help my anger, though…or my half-hard dick. I dry my face with a paper towel and glance in the mirror, pushing my dark brown hair out of my face.

Will everyone in this town always think of me as nothing more than the party boy with a shit ton of bad habits? I get that I may have hurt some people around here. That's why I left and went to Nashville. I didn't move back until I had my shit together, and I've been clean ever since. Maybe the past is just too much to outrun.

Deciding to stop my pity party, I head out of the bathroom and back to the bar. I see Courtney sitting back in her seat, nursing her drink and pouting.

My eyes glance around to the other side of the bar, and I stop dead in my tracks.

*Tracy Kennedy.*

I've seen Tracy since I've gotten back, but we've never uttered more than a cookie-cutter greeting to one another. Maybe there's a reason for that.

Tracy Kennedy was the first person in this world I could call a best friend. Hell, she might be the only person ever truly to fit that bill.

We met our first day of Kindergarten and were inseparable from that day forward. There was barely a day that went by that we weren't together. We were thick as thieves...until our last year of high school. That's when everything changed. Needless to say, when you introduce sex into any relationship, let alone a friendship, things can get messy.

*And not in a good way.*

I've always had regrets about how we left things. After all, she was my dream girl.

And now, I see she's just as beautiful as ever. Her wavy auburn-colored hair hangs to her shoulders. There's a smattering of freckles over her nose and cheeks. Her skin has always been tan from all the time she spends outside and now is no different.

She looks like she's wearing a little bit of makeup which *is* different for her. At least it used to be. Tracy was never much for girly things.

But maybe she's not that same girl she was all those years ago.

She hasn't noticed me yet, so I take a moment just to let my mind remember everything we used to have. I wish I could say I've thought about her more before this very moment, but I've been pretty selfish the past few years, and I'm sure thinking about my first love would have just made me feel guilty.

I could stand here and stare at her all night, but when her big, round, green eyes finally find mine, I know my time of watching from a distance is over.

She sees me, and a smile hits her lips. It's just as genuine and heart-warming as I remember, but it's also a little nervous and unsure.

My own grin immediately follows as I walk over to her. Then, when there's nothing but a bar-top in between the two of us, I lean my elbows on the polished wood so that I'm eye-level with her.

"Well, well," I say. "As I live and breathe, Miss Tracy Kennedy."

With just two words, her voice seems to bring up every memory we ever shared.

"Hi, Jessie."

# Chapter Three

## TRACY

"Hi, Jessie."

That's all I can manage to get out because just being near him again, my brain has gone into overload. Jessie Mitchell stands in front of me, and he seems just as handsome and charming as ever.

When we were younger, I couldn't imagine life without him. Our lives were so intricately woven together. And one day, it all just went away. In the blink of an eye, I lost my best friend and my first love all at once.

Things got so messy that I'm not even entirely sure what happened. Or maybe I've just blocked it all out. Being seventeen and losing one of the most important people in my life makes for a damn good excuse to try to forget.

Now that he's looking at me, it feels as though none of that should matter.

But it does.

"It's been a long time," he begins. "I've been back in town for a while. Figured we would have caught up before now."

"You knew where to find me," I say, a little snarkier than I mean to.

But he is still smiling. "Back at you, T."

My stomach somersaults at the nickname he gave to me when we were kids. He's the only person ever to call me T.

"I've come into the bar before," I retort.

He chuckles. "You came in once, and you were with Andi. And if I remember correctly, you didn't stay long or so much as give me a sideways glance."

I remember the night he's talking about. My best friend, Andi, was in a fight with her now-husband and was looking to drown her sorrows. I met her here but was careful to avoid any interaction with Jessie.

Although I was trying to escape a painfully uncomfortable situation, it isn't as bad as I imagined now that we're here. He stares at me with his baby blues. Every one of the Mitchell kids has those piercing eyes.

We gaze at each other. Both of us seeming like we have so much to say, but neither of us uttering a word.

Just when Jessie opens his mouth to speak, someone at the other end of the bar gets his attention.

"One second," he says to me, hurrying over to fulfill their order.

I watch him make drink orders with ease and handle the Friday night crowd.

When we graduated high school, Jessie moved to Nashville. He was always anxious to get out of this small town. When he left, it made it so much easier to move on and pretend that he didn't exist. Now that he's back, it's not quite that simple.

When I look at him, I see the boy who I played Hide and Seek with all around this town. I see the boy who held me while I cried when my mom died. And I see the boy who looked at me with all the love in the world as we lost our virginity to each other.

Now, he's grown even more handsome than he once was. His dark hair is slightly longer on top than it used to be. He's taller than he once was but still has a lean figure.

My eyes continue to follow Jessie until I see a pretty blonde at the end of the bar who hasn't taken her eyes off of him.

*Neither have I, so who am I to judge?*

When he finally makes his way back over to me, I nod in

the direction of the blonde and ask, "What's with Tits McGee over there?"

He doesn't need to look over to know who I'm talking about. "She wanted to have some fun, but I politely declined."

My eyes go wide. "You didn't want to take a turn on that ride?"

He laughs. "I forgot that you don't hold back. I would have gladly taken a turn, but let's just say that she was trying to have the kind of fun that I'm trying to stay away from."

Remembering that he's trying to stay out of trouble, I simply nod. Trying to lighten the conversation, I say, "Look at you... still the ultimate ladies man."

He rolls his eyes. "Not as much as you may think." He dries a couple of glasses as he talks. "Besides, I'm guessing you had a date tonight."

He points at me, moving his finger up and down. I look down at the dress that I'm wearing, well aware it's a far cry from my usual tank tops and cut-off shorts.

He adds. "Don't get me wrong; you look gorgeous with the makeup and everything. But, then again, you never needed any of that to be gorgeous."

My cheeks heat at his compliment. Trying to play it off, I smirk and reply, "Man, you're still just a charmer. Some things never change, huh?"

His face turns serious. "Yeah, but some things do."

*Damn, he's sure right about that.*

The way he looks at me, though, transports me right back to our past.

In this moment, everything has changed, yet nothing feels different.

He flashes me his million-watt smile before someone else needs his attention. Then, as he walks away, I find it hard to breathe, as though the air in here is slowly being sucked out.

I'm beyond flustered with myself because I am *not* this girl. I'm a girl who takes shit from no one—the girl who is independent as hell and lives life on her own terms. I'm not the girl who lets a man get inside her head.

Realizing I need to get my thoughts in order...and get some fucking air...I throw a twenty on the bar and head for the door.

After seven years, I think that's enough of Jessie Mitchell for one night.

# Chapter Four

## JESSIE

When I go back to continue my conversation with Tracy, she's gone. I don't know if I said something wrong or if it was all just too heavy.

The rest of my shift flies by in a chaotic blur. I keep busy making drinks and cleaning as I go, which makes closing time a little easier. But, although my hands keep working, my mind is a hundred miles away.

All I can think about is Tracy. My mind gets wrapped up in a sea of memories.

Even back then…even when we were just kids…I felt like we were soulmates. Call me crazy, but I was drawn to her, unlike any other girl I've ever been around. And as my oldest brother likes to say, "When you know, you just know." Even as a kid, I just knew.

Tracy Kennedy was like a wildflower--absolutely beautiful but impossible to try to contain. She thrived off of sunshine and bare feet. Fire flowed through her veins as she took the world by storm. There was no one quite like her, and I was entranced from day one.

She viewed the world in such a unique way. Even after her momma died, she still was so optimistic about life. And un-like most people in small towns, she wasn't itching to get out. Grady was her home, and instead of yearning for the big city, she wanted to always live in Grady and do her part to help the community that she grew up in.

I, on the other hand, was always intrigued by the fast pace of the big city. That was probably the only thing we ever disagreed on.

I guess the joke is on me, though, because I *did* leave Grady for the big city, and all it gave me was an even worse drug problem and some of the worst memories of my life.

By the time I leave the bar, I feel mentally exhausted yet wide awake all at the same time. I hop in the driver's seat of my old pick-up truck and light a cigarette before starting the engine.

The drive back to my place is a short one, and I try to finish smoking by the time I get there. Currently, I'm staying at the rental house on my oldest brother's cattle ranch. Usually, I wouldn't want to live mere steps from Jonas Mitchell, who seems to always have something to say about my life choices. But it beats living with my momma, which is what I was doing when I first got back into town.

Ever since Jonas met his wife, Andi, and they became foster parents to two little boys, he's mellowed some. He's not quite as much of a hard-ass, but I'm still not in the mood to hear him bitch about my smoking.

When I pull up in the driveway that runs between our two houses, I see that Jonas is sitting outside on his large wraparound porch. He's drinking a beer and rocking on one of the porch swings.

Knowing that it's after one in the morning, I figure something has to be wrong. I'm tempted to go directly inside, but instead, I walk over to check on my brother.

"Hey." He nods at me as I walk up the steps onto his porch. "How was work?"

Jonas has never tried to hide the fact that he thinks me working at a bar is a terrible idea, so I appreciate him asking.

"It was Karaoke Night. What do you think?" I quip.

"The offer still stands for you to come work at the ranch."

*There it is.*

Jonas always offers me a job, but he and I mix together about as well as oil and water. I'm not sure I can spend every day taking orders from him.

I just scoff and change the subject. "So, why are you up so late? You're usually sawing logs by the time I get home from work."

He takes another long swig of beer. "Kyle had another one of those night terror things." Kyle is the eldest of their foster kids. He's eight, I think.

I remember Andi mentioning something about him having trouble sleeping, but I don't know the whole story.

"Night terrors?" I ask.

"Vivid, awful nightmares. Before the boys came to us, I guess some rough shit happened at their last foster home. Sometimes, he dreams about it. He starts screaming bloody murder, so Andi goes in to calm him down. Usually, she can fall back asleep pretty quickly, but I get so rattled that it takes me forever. So, I decided to come out here for some air."

"That's some rough shit, man. I'm sorry."

He shrugs. "Comes with the territory, I guess."

"How's Andi handling everything?" I ask, referring to the fact that Andi grew up in the foster system as well.

"Like a saint. You know Andi—she's amazing at everything she does. Except cooking—she still can't do that to save her life."

We both laugh before hearing, "I heard that."

Andi comes walking outside onto the porch with her wild black curls flying everywhere and a sleepy look on her face. Walking over to her husband, she sits on his lap, resting her head against his chest.

"Was I interrupting something?" She asks.

"Nope," we both reply in unison.

"Okay, then." She yawns. "In that case, let's go to bed, cowboy."

*That's my cue.*

I begin to walk away when I hear my brother say, "Don't

21

forget tomorrow is Keith's birthday party."

"Already took the day off. I wouldn't miss it."

As I walk off, I can hear my brother telling his wife how much he loves her. I'd be lying if I said I wasn't a little jealous of what they have. It must be nice to have someone who's always in your corner. Someone who celebrates your successes and picks you up after your failures. Someone to be your true partner.

There have only been two times in my life that I've ever felt like that. Once was with Tracy, and although I don't remember all the details of what happened, I'm sure I was the one who fucked it up.

The other was Gabby. She and I hooked up when I was in Nashville. She was just as messed up in the head as I was. She was my partner in crime, but in the worst way imaginable. When I got clean, she didn't, and before I left, things got far worse than I ever dreamed they would.

I left for my own self-preservation. I genuinely believe that if I had stayed, one of us would have ended up dead. I try to push those thoughts from my head. Coming back to Grady was my opportunity for a fresh start, so I shouldn't dwell on the past too much.

When I get inside my house, I walk over and grab a water bottle out of the fridge. Still trapped in my own head, I wish I had something stronger than water to drink. Although alcohol was never one of my vices, when I went clean, I gave up everything that impaired my judgment. It's not easier to remember my past mistakes constantly, but it keeps me from making some new ones.

The choice to stay clean is one that I have to make every day, and some of those days are more of a struggle than others.

There's one constant that always reminds me, though—despite how unhealthy a habit it may be.

Taking a seat on the couch, I open the small wooden box that sits on the end table. My fingers grip the small photo that's in it.

When I pull it out, I take a long, hard look at it, and it's obvious why it's so crucial for me to stay on the right track.

My eyes focus on the image in front of them for what feels like hours.

The image that keeps me on the right track.

The image that changed my life.

The image that shows the sonogram of my son.

# Chapter Five

### TRACY

"So, what exactly goes on at a kid's birthday party?" I ask. "Does a stripper jump out of the cake later?"

My best friend, Andi, throws her head back, laughing. "Yes, Trace. That's *exactly* what happens. And then, we give all the kids dollar bills to shove in her g-string."

"It's a girl stripper? Oh, well then, I'm out of here," I joke.

"Oh, shut up and help me carry these party trays outside."

We each grab one of the large trays covered in snacks and head out the back door into the yard. Tables are set up all over the lawn, and I wonder how many people are coming to this thing.

"Look at you doing the whole 'mom' thing," I say.

She smiles back at me. "Well, I'm trying. It's definitely an adjustment, but I'm so happy we could take the boys and give them a good home. Sometimes, I wonder though if we are just going to end up messing them up even worse."

I shake my head. "Impossible. You and Jonas are the two best people I know. Those boys are going to grow up with more love than they know what to do with."

It might sound cheesy, but it's the damn truth. Jonas and Andi were made for each other. Andi moved from California to Grady less than a year ago. She moved into the smaller house on the ranch, and it wasn't long before she and Jonas were madly in love.

We set the trays on one of the tables and walk back inside to grab another.

"Did you make the food?" I ask. The question makes us both laugh since everyone knows Andi can't cook worth a damn. I love her to death, but anything requiring more than a microwave isn't for her.

'No, smartass. Nicole made the food."

Nicole used to be engaged to Jonas. Now, we are all friends, and Andi is even helping Nicole start her own catering business. Nicole also helps me do some modeling for my clothing store since she's gorgeous.

In a town as small as Grady, there's a lot of overlap.

"Didn't you have a date last night?" Andi asks. "How'd that go?"

I groan. "About as well as your cooking."

"That bad, huh?"

"The worst." I sigh. "I don't know why everyone insists that I need to find a man. I mean, do I have the word 'desperate' written on my forehead? I'm doing just fine on my own."

"Of course, you are. Just because being alone is alright, though, doesn't mean that is the only way to live."

My eyes roll. "Oh no, not you too."

Her hands fly up. "Hey, I haven't tried to set you up with anyone. I'm just saying if love comes knocking, don't avoid it, or you might miss out on something wonderful. I almost made that mistake with Jonas. Besides, don't you want someone around who can make your toes curl?"

I shrug. "Sure. But I have yet to find a man who can make me come like a vibrator. And my battery-powered boyfriend doesn't annoy me or ask me where his dinner is."

She giggles. "Fair enough."

When we get back outside, I see more people starting to file in and sit down at different tables. Then, I stop abruptly when I see Jessie Mitchell.

Clearing my throat, I look to Andi. "Jessie's here?"

"Well, yeah. He *is* Jonas's brother, which makes him uncle to the boys."

*Duh. How did I forget that?*

"Right," I mutter.

"Why? What's wrong with that?" She asks. "Are you still doing the whole avoiding him thing?"

"No. Sort of. I don't know. I went to The Saddle last night."

Her eyes go wide. "You *never* go to The Saddle. Tell me everything."

"Nothing to tell, really. I stopped by for a beer after my shitty date. He was tending bar."

"And?"

"And...we talked. It was only slightly awkward. It was just...I don't know." I stammer.

"Trace, when are you going to tell me what happened between the two of you?"

I wave off the question. "It's a long story."

"Who says we don't have time now?"

As if right on cue, her youngest son comes running up to us, "Andi!"

"We're at your kid's birthday party," I whisper with a smirk.

"Right." She laughs and walks away to deal with whatever problem Keith is having.

I busy myself rearranging the food trays on the table. I have no idea what I'm doing, but it beats standing around doing nothing.

Occasionally, my eyes drift over to where Jessie sits. Now, the rest of the Mitchell clan has joined him. Jonas is the oldest son, and Jared is next in line. Both of them have dirty blonde hair and light blue eyes. Jonas has wavy hair, while Jared's is straight and pulled back into a man bun.

Next in line is Jessie, who has darker hair than the rest. And rounding them out is Jenna, who is still in high school. Also sitting at the table is Jared's daughter, Macey, and the matriarch of the entire family, Annie.

Annie Mitchell is the sweetest woman on the face of the Earth. She was there for my dad and me when my mom died, and she's always been wonderful to me, even when Jessie and I had our falling out.

She now brings Jenna into the store to shop from time to time, and I always make sure to give her a hefty discount.

When I was younger, I loved spending time with Jessie at the Mitchell house. After my mom died, it was just my dad and me. I loved every second I spent with my dad, but there was something I craved about the chaos of a big family. And I always felt like Annie treated me like one of her own.

My attention is drawn away when a couple of older women walk over to the table I'm standing at. Brenda Jenkins is the town gossip, and her friend, Marlow Woodard, is one of her little goons.

Brenda and I stare at each other for a few moments, locked in a silent stand-off before I reluctantly move out of the way.

Marlow chuckles, and I just smirk. I know that Marlow has been cheating on her husband with a guy twenty years younger than she is.

How do I know this? She lives across the street from me, and I see things I really wish I didn't.

I step to the side and grab a bottle of water out of the cooler.

Brenda turns to Marlow. "Can you believe that the youngest Mitchell boy has the nerve to show his face around this town again?"

Marlow shakes her head. "We all knew he was going to turn out just like that dead-beat daddy of his."

Brenda adds, "Annie had four kids with that no-good son-of-a-bitch. One of them was bound to get his horrible genes."

Marlow chuckles. "No one has ever accused Annie Mitchell of being smart."

My blood boils, and I can't keep my mouth shut any longer. "You two old hags talk a lot of shit for women who have enough skeletons in their closet to fill a cemetery."

Wide-eyed, they both turn their attention to me, but before they can utter a single syllable, I walk away.

Jessie and I may have had our share of drama, but I'll never be okay with anyone talking shit about him or his family behind their backs.

Walking over to one of the still-empty tables, I take a seat. My eyes scan the people to try to find Andi, but no luck. The kids have all gathered in a group and are running around shooting each other with water guns. Their cries are ear-piercing as they fly past me.

*Holy hell, this is going to be a long day.*

# Chapter Six

### JESSIE

"Everyone is staring at me," I grumble. "I swear I can hear them talking trash from here.

My momma rolls her eyes. "No one is staring at you. You're paranoid."

My teenage sister, Jenna, speaks up. "No, he's right. Everyone's staring."

My mom crumples up her napkin and tosses it at her daughter. "Jenna Leigh, stop it!"

Jenna rolls her eyes. "Mom, you shouldn't lie to him. Everybody's been talking about Jessie since he got back to town."

Momma gasps. "Well, what are they saying?"

Jenna starts picking at her nails. "That he's just like Daddy. That the only time anyone sees him is when he tends bar a few nights a week. That they think it's super weird that any other time, he's nowhere to be found."

Now, I interrupt. "Why on Earth would I want to be around people who constantly bad-mouth me?"

My momma chuckles. "It seems like a double-edged sword. They talk about you when you don't come around, and they talk about you when you do."

I scoff. "That's why it's just easier to stay away. At least then, I don't have to hear the whispers."

Jenna says, "My point is that everyone thinks you're still

29

a drug addict. Maybe if you showed your face more, people wouldn't assume that. Unless you're hiding something…"

"Jenna Leigh Mitchell!" My mother scolds.

"Whatever," my sister mutters under her breath before getting up and stomping off.

Jared stands up to follow her. "I got it." As he's walking away, he sarcastically adds, "Man, I can't wait for Macey to be a teenager."

Once they're out of ear-shot, my momma sets her hand on mine. "You know, you really need to make things right with that girl."

I rub my eyes. "Yeah, she should get in line. Apparently, there are a lot of people who I've disappointed over the years."

"Don't you think your sister should be at the top of the list to make amends with?"

*Probably.*

Not ready to admit that, though, I respond, "I get that I'm a fuck-up…"

Momma interrupts me with a smack to my shoulder. "Language!"

"Sorry. Yes, I'm a *screw-up,* but I don't think I ever really did anything to her. I mean, I was awful to you and Jonas, and both of you forgave me. What did I even do to Jenna?"

She sighs. "You left. Just when you two started getting closer, you graduated high school and skipped town. And then, you get back and move in with us. She was looking forward to spending time with you again. And then, you move onto the ranch with Jonas."

"I'm not living with Jonas, Momma. I'm living in his rental by myself. That was the whole point—*to be by myself.*"

"I know that, and you know that. But, that doesn't mean that Jeanna gets it. You know teenagers can't see more than two feet in front of their own faces. Just make things right with her. Your daddy wasn't ever around for her."

I grit my teeth. "I'm getting tired of everyone comparing me to that man."

She begins, "You know that's not what…"

But I hold my hand up. "I know. It's fine. I think I'm just going to take a walk."

She opens her mouth to say something else but decides against it. I shove my hands in my pockets and head toward the dirt path that leads back further onto the ranch.

I feel like a dick for leaving the party, but my being there didn't seem to be helping anything. Needless to say, I don't think anyone was paying attention to Keith when the town fuck-up decided to show his face.

I thought coming back to Grady would be great for me, but now I wonder if I'll ever truly be able to escape my past. My feet continue to carry me back further onto the property.

It leads into a thicket of trees, but I know exactly where I'm going. I haven't been in years, but it's probably my favorite place in the whole world.

When I reach my destination, I'm immediately transported back in time.

# Chapter Seven

### JESSIE

*Thirteen years ago.*

"Slow down, T!" I call after my best friend.

She slows down from a run to a brisk walk before turning back to me and smiling.

"Remind me again why we're running through the woods?" I ask.

She puts her arm around my shoulders. "Because these woods are the only place in Grady that we haven't explored."

She's got a point, but I still don't know why we're running.

"Don't you just love the woods?" She says, sticking her nose up in the air, sniffing. "Do you smell that?"

I mimic her in sniffing the air. "Smell what?"

Her head snaps toward me, and there's a new twinkle in her eye. She smirks. "Water."

In a flash, she takes off once more. This time, pulling my arm, forcing me to keep up with her.

We run for about a minute before she stops unexpectedly, and I slam into the back of her.

"Ow...what the—?" I don't finish my thought because I see what made her stop.

In the middle of these woods is a small lake. The sun shines down on it, making it look like the water is sparkling. Lilly pads and pretty flowers line the outside of the lake's edge.

It looks like something you'd see on a painting…or one of those jigsaw puzzles my granddaddy always does.

Tracy smugly smiles at the fact that her super-sniffer was right on the money.

I look at her. "You're like a bloodhound. Do you know that?"

She just rolls her green eyes at me. "You're just jealous."

Before I can think of a witty comeback, she's already racing off toward the water's edge. She's running so fast I expect her to jump right in.

But she doesn't. She stops right on the bank and sits down.

Looking over at her, I can see the sun illuminating the freckles on her nose and cheeks. She hates the tiny dots, but I think they're cute. If I called Tracy cute, though, she'd probably kick my ass. She's spunky like that.

We are quiet as we look out over the calm water. It's beautiful.

"I wish we could stay here forever," she finally says.

"Me too. But I'm sure you'd get hungry after a while. Well, sooner rather than later."

She laughs. "I know how to fish."

That's true. And she's way better at it than I am.

The way she looks at this place, though, makes me never want to leave either. But the sun's starting to set, and I know Momma will be mad as heck if I'm not home for dinner.

"Hey, T," I say.

Without looking at me, she responds, "Yeah, Jessie?"

"How about you and I make a promise?"

That gets her to make eye contact finally.

I continue. "We don't tell anyone about this place. We keep it a secret for just us. So it can be our special place."

She takes a moment to think it over before looking at me and grinning.

"Deal."

# Chapter Eight

## TRACY

I've learned something today. Children's birthday parties are painfully dull for adults. Andi's been so busy that I've been hanging out by myself most of the day.

My eyes kept drifting over to Jessie's table. I wasn't close enough to hear what was being said, but I watched Jenna get mad and storm off as Jared follows her. Then, it looked like Jessie and his mom had a heated discussion before he got up and walked away too.

He was gone for about half an hour before I decided to go after him.

So now, I follow the dirt path further into the wood. I know precisely where Jessie is heading. It's the same place we went to thousands of times in our childhood—especially when things got rough.

I don't know if the lake ever actually had a name. Jessie and I always referred to it as Lake TJ—an homage to both of our names.

It was our happy place for pretty much our entire childhood. But I haven't been back in years.

One, because Jonas Mitchell bought the land, so technically, it's *his* lake now.

And two, it's always been full of memories. Memories that were easier to try to forget than admit they were some of the best times of my life.

When I see the trees beginning to clear up ahead, those memories flood my thoughts.

Once I emerge, I see Jessie is sitting on a dock that leads out into the water. I figure Jonas must have had the dock built for him to fish on.

Seeming trapped in his own thoughts, Jessie hasn't noticed me yet. It's only when a twig cracks under my foot that his head snaps my way.

It takes less than a second for a big smile to spread across his lips. "Hey, T. What are you doing out here?'

Taking a seat next to him, I respond, "I could ask you the same thing. Aren't you supposed to be at your nephew's birthday party?"

He sighs. "I'm supposed to be, but it seemed like everyone was more focused on me than on Keith."

"When did you begin giving a shit what other people thought about you? You and I used to give the haters a big middle finger."

He chuckles. "That was all you. I just fell in line."

"Well, time to fall in line now." I smile. "Screw all those jerks."

He's quiet for a moment before he says, "They all think I'm just like my dad."

Jessie's dad, John, was the talk of the town for years. After getting hurt at the factory he worked at, he got hooked on painkillers before moving onto alcohol. Annie put up with it for a while, but when John moved onto harder drugs, she made him leave. Every so often, he'd come back home, seemingly clean and sober. He'd make a ton of promises about how things would be different. And they would be for a while. Then, he'd slip back into his old ways, breaking everyone's hearts in the process.

It's true that I haven't spent time with Jessie in years, but I know without a doubt that Jessie is *not* his father. The fact that he is trying to better himself makes him worlds apart from John.

I set my hand on top of his, and it's like there's a spark that jolts through me at the contact.

His eyes flick down to my hand on his, and a whisper of a smile falls on his lips. "Look at you, T. All these years later, and you still have my back...even after...everything."

"I can't help it. You just always seem to need protecting," I joke. "Ever since Kindergarten."

We both laugh at the memory of the first time we met. It was our first day of Kindergarten, and some boys were giving Jessie a hard time about who his daddy was. When he tried to ignore them, they pushed him down and started kicking him. Before they got that far, I pulled one of them off and punched him square in the nose. The others got scared and ran away. I helped Jessie up, and we were inseparable after that.

After my trip down memory lane, I say, "Jess, my point is that you're not your dad. Sure, you fucked up. Who doesn't do that every once in a while? Don't be so hard on yourself. Just pick yourself up by your bootstraps and try to do better."

He smiles and shakes his head. "You really haven't changed, have you?"

I shrug. "Oh, I've changed. Just not any of the important things."

I take my hand off his and immediately miss the contact.

Kicking off my boots, I scoot closer to the end of the dock and dangle my feet into the cool water.

"What are you doing?" Jessie asks.

"What does it look like I'm doing? Do you want to join me?"

He follows suit and scoots closer, taking his own boots off.

As his toes hit the water, he lets out a shriek while yanking his knees back toward him. "Holy shit, that's freezing!"

My laugh echoes off the trees. "Don't be a baby. It's not that cold."

Slowly, he lowers his feet until his toes sink into the water once more. He makes funny noises the whole time, and I can't stop laughing.

"You think this is funny?" He smiles.

I hold my fingers close together. "Just a little bit. I remember way back when I would have dove head first into that cold water, and you would've been right behind me doing it too."

He nods, and a piece of his chestnut hair falls into his eyes. "True. But that's because I was following you. I would have followed you anywhere."

Without even thinking about it, I respond, "Well, not *anywhere.*"

Awkwardness falls between us for what feels like an eternity. It's as though everything we want to say to each other is hanging in the air, but neither of us wants to speak the first words.

And instead of saying them now, Jessie changes the subject. "So, what have you been up to the past few years?"

"Oh, not too much."

"Really?" His eyebrows raise. "I hear you've got a hell of a business going."

"I mean, I'm not lying in a bathtub made of gold counting my money, but I do alright."

He chuckles. "Fair enough. But for what it's worth, it's awesome what you've accomplished. Be proud of yourself. I sure as hell am."

I smile but don't respond. I've never been one to handle compliments well. Despite my adventurous spirit, I don't like the spotlight being on me.

"What about you?" I change the subject yet again. "Do you want to talk about what happened when you were in Nashville?"

His eyes stay fixed on the glassy water. "T, as much as I do want to tell you about it, this place is too magical for a story like that."

I want to tell him that's bullshit because this place has seen us through some of the worst times. Hell, this is where I ran to when my momma died.

But I don't say that. "This place really is beautiful, isn't it?"

He looks around. "It sure is. I was just thinking about when we first found this place. Do you remember?"

"Of course! How could I forget? We made a promise never to tell anyone about it. And then your brother up and buys the land that it sits on. Quite the coincidence, huh?" I smirk.

"Yeah, I kind of fucked up on that one. But if it makes you feel any better, I didn't actually tell him. One day, I came out here to be alone, and Jonas and Jared followed me."

I nod. "Makes sense. I figured it was something like that. Do you still come out here now that Jonas owns it?"

"Nope. Ever since the day my brothers found it, I've never been back. You weren't here anymore, and I guess it kind of lost something for me."

"And now that you're back?"

He smiles. "Well, you're back here with me, so maybe the magic isn't as lost as I thought it was."

Being here with Jessie feels so...comfortable. I've always kept my circle small, and I don't let many people get close to me. But, despite all we went through, I don't know that Jessie will ever *not* be part of that circle.

As wonderful as it is to have my friend back, though, letting go of the pain and the hurt may not be an easy feat.

We spend the next couple of hours just talking. Mainly, it's about nothing at all, but it's nice all the same. For a little while, we don't dwell on the past or worry about the nosy townspeople.

When the sun is beginning to set, I suggest that we better be heading back.

"Do we have to?" He asks.

"We should before they send out a search party."

"Oh yeah, I'm sure the tongues are wagging like crazy seeing me walk off into the woods with Tracy Kennedy following behind. There are probably already a dozen sordid stories about what we are doing out here."

I shrug. "Let them talk. Gossip doesn't bother me. Besides, I have so much dirt on everyone here in Grady, I don't think they'll be pissing me off."

Our feet have dried by now, so we put our boots back on before standing up.

Slowly, we walk back to the path. Before stepping onto it, Jessie grabs my hand.

"Wait," he says, "Before we go, let's make another promise."

"You want to break another one?" I joke.

"Okay, smart ass. Let's promise each other that this won't be the last time we come here."

I think for a moment, trying to decide if I really am ready to open this can of worms again. Am I ready to let all of these emotions back in?

But ultimately, it doesn't take long for me to decide.

"Deal."

# Chapter Nine

JESSIE

"You know you really shouldn't smoke those," Tracy tells me as I light the cigarette I just stuck in my mouth.

"You sound like Jonas," I scoff.

"Maybe if more than one person is telling you that, you should listen."

"Are you going to give me the whole speech about how smoking is bad and can kill me?"

She smirks at me. "I was going to tell you that maybe some women wouldn't want to kiss a man after you smoke one of those."

She walks a couple of steps ahead of me on the trail, allowing me to catch a glimpse of her ass. Tracy has always been relatively petite. Back in the day, she was flat as a board. Then, when we hit puberty, her chest stayed small, but her ass and hips got bigger—which I loved. I'm an ass man, remember?

My eyes stay glued to her cut-off shorts that show off her round backside.

"Stop staring at my ass," she quips.

"I can't help it. It's a great ass."

Now, she turns around to look at me. "You're still just as smooth as ever, aren't you?"

"Nah, I haven't had much practice lately."

She slows her pace so that we are side-by-side yet again. "I highly doubt that. I'm sure women still flock to you. They always did."

"Not so much anymore. Not that I've really been out there looking, though."

"Why's that?" She asks.

My shoulders shrug. "Most of the places I would normally go to find dates, I now tend to stay away from. And if I do meet women, they're usually the kind that are no good for me. Trying to stay out of trouble isn't great for my sex life."

"You could always try online dating," she suggests.

"Is that what you do?"

She laughs. "I tried a couple of times. Didn't really go well."

"Exactly," I sigh. "Maybe I'm just waiting on the right girl to walk back into my life."

I wonder if she catches my attempt at a subtle hint. The way she's hiding a slight smile tells me she does.

"So, do you have to work tomorrow?" I ask, trying to break the sudden tension.

"No, on Sundays, I usually go over to help my dad."

"How's Abe doing?" Tracy's dad was always a stand-up guy who always treated me with nothing but respect.

"He's as good as can be expected. A few years back, he had a heart attack, and the doc told him he needed to slow down. So, he sold most of the farmland. Now, he grows just enough for some local folks."

"I can't believe someone told Abe Kennedy to slow down, and he actually listened."

She laughs. "Oh, trust me, he wasn't happy about it. The man who was 98% steak and cheeseburgers had to cut out red meat. He isn't supposed to do anything strenuous either, so I go over one or two days a week to help. He hates it, but after I flipped out on him for being so careless, he finally started to listen."

The mental image of little Tracy putting her larger-than-life father in his place is hilarious. But then again, I'd expect

41

nothing less from her.

You know how they say most women are fragile like flowers? Tracy Kennedy is fragile like a bomb.

She can be sweet as molasses, but the moment you piss her off, she will make you wish you were never born.

We keep walking as the sun sets. She tells me more about her dad and her business. Then, she asks me about my momma.

"Oh, Annie Mitchell is just as perfect as ever. I swear the only thing that woman has ever done wrong is marrying my no-good daddy."

"But if she hadn't married him, she wouldn't have had you guys."

"Yeah, but it sure would have saved her a whole hell of a lot of heartache. Maybe I should rephrase and say that her mistake was taking him back all those times."

Her fingertips wrap around my arm before she says, "Jessie, your momma has always been one to try to see the good in everyone. Don't ever try to take that away from her. It's a rare quality to have, especially after everything she's been through."

I nod. "You're right. I just wish she hadn't had to deal with all of that through the years."

She gives me a weak smile before taking her hand off my arm. "I know. But life goes on, right?"

My memory flashes back to when Tracy's mom died. We were only about 8 or 9 at the time, and she said those exact same words.

*Life goes on, right?*

She said them with a fake smile plastered on her lips as if her world hadn't just imploded on her.

That was Tracy, though. Ride the wind wherever it takes her. But when a storm rolls in, it knocks her for a loop.

We continue to catch up as we slowly make our way back to the front of the ranch where the party was going on. But by the time we reach the clearing, it looks like everyone has gone home. All the tables are empty, and all the chairs are put up. The only sign that there was even a party here is the giant bounce house, which is still inflated.

Tracy is ahead of me, and when she abruptly stops, I slam into the back of her.

She turns back to look at me with a big smile and wide eyes and says, "You want to do something fun?"

Man, those words got us into so much trouble when we were kids.

She grabs my hand and takes off at a full-fledged sprint. I take pride in the shape I'm in. I'm pretty fit, and I work out quite a bit, but Tracy is quick as a bullet shot out of a pistol. I struggle to keep up with her even though my legs are longer.

She stops right in front of the bounce house. With a gleam in her eye, she kicks off her boots and climbs through the mesh door.

"Come on, wild child," she taunts.

I can't help but laugh as I slip out of my boots. "I'm pretty sure that was *your* nickname back in the day," I say, crawling in after her.

"True. But I think it's more fitting for you these days."

"Says the girl who just climbed in a children's bounce house," I mumble under my breath.

"I heard that."

She's already bouncing as high as she can go, making it almost impossible for me to stand up. Every time I try, I fall right back down.

"Stop bouncing," I plead through my laughter.

But she doesn't stop. Instead, she just keeps teasing. "You okay there, Jess? Do you need a hand? You look like you need some help."

My stomach hurts from laughing so hard.

Finally, her bouncing stops, and she holds out her hand to help me up. But the second our hands lock, I playfully yank her down to the floor next to me.

As quickly as I can, I stand up and start bouncing, giving her a taste of her own medicine.

She giggles as her tiny body bounces up and down like a

piece of popcorn flying around in the heat.

"If you don't stop, I swear I'm going to laugh so hard that I wet myself," she cries.

I finally stop and help her up. "We wouldn't want that now, would we? That's not exactly the kind of *wet* that I'd want to make you."

Our eyes meet, and something passes between us, but before either one of us can speak, we hear the backdoor to the house creak open.

Jonas comes stepping out onto his porch. "Someone out there?" He calls.

"Jonas will kill us," I whisper.

Backing me into a corner, Tracy puts her hand over my mouth. She works her bottom lip between her teeth as we both listen.

"I know you're out here," he says, this time a little louder.

I hear his boots walking across the porch and down the steps. We both hold our breath as he gets closer.

My brother already thinks I'm a troublemaker, and this isn't going to help matters.

Just when I'm sure we're about to get busted, the back door swings open again, but this time, it's Andi that we hear.

"Joe, what are you doing?"

He answers. "I thought I heard someone out here."

"Oh Jonas, there's no one out here. We're in the middle of nowhere. Come in and help give these boys their baths."

"Okay, baby," he says as his footsteps head back toward the house.

Only when he's inside, and the door closes behind him, do we both release the breaths we've been holding.

As she looks up at me with those big green eyes, there's so much that I want to say to her. I want to apologize for letting our relationship fall apart. I want to ask for her forgiveness. I want to admit that if I kept her by my side, that I probably wouldn't have fucked up as much as I did. And I want to beg her for another chance because the short amount of time I've spent with her, the past couple of days have made me feel more alive than I have in years.

But before I can say any of that, she stands on her tip-toes and kisses me on the cheek.

When she pulls back, she's got a massive smile on her face. "Thanks, Wild Child."

With that, she slides out of the entrance to the bounce house, grabs her boots, and takes off running toward her car, which is parked a little way down the road.

I watch her the entire time until she finally gets in her Jeep and drives off. Then, I begin making my way back to the rental, trying to make as little noise as possible.

When I'm safely inside, I set my boots by the door and flop on the couch. My mind floods with thoughts of Tracy. I'd forgotten how amazing she is. I should've known the second I was near her again, she'd pull me in like a magnetic force.

Maybe that's why I stayed away.

But now that we're both here, I'm not letting this opportunity pass us by.

Out of habit, I reach into the small box next to the couch and pull out the same tattered photo I always stare at.

My nightly reminder of how I refuse to repeat my past mistakes and how I want a different future.

For almost a year, it's been my only reason.

But tonight, I don't stare at it for quite so long. Because tonight, I realize maybe I have more than one reason.

# Chapter Ten

## TRACY

*Nine years ago.*

"What do you want to do tonight, T?" Jessie asks me.

I shove a handful of sunflower seeds into my mouth and shrug my shoulders. "We could go see a movie."

"Eh, I don't know. That's almost a two-hour ride on our bikes to get to the closest theatre."

"I could steal my daddy's truck, and we could go to the drive-in," I offer.

"Hell no! Remember how mad he got last time? He just about skinned us both," he cries.

But I just wave him off. "You're being dramatic. He was too. I mean, what's the big deal? I didn't wreck it, did I?"

"Maybe he had a problem with it since neither of us has a driver's license."

I shrug again. "We both only have a couple of months before we get them."

"True. All the same, let's just not do anything to make your daddy mad."

"Fine. Then, what's your big, bright idea for what to do tonight?" I ask.

"Want to get some snacks and take them down to the lake?"

Without answering, I stand up and begin walking.

"Is that a yes?" He calls.

I nod. "You had me at snacks."

An hour later, we're on the bank of the lake, full on all of the junk food we brought.

We're quiet for a little while before Jessie asks, "You ever think about the future?"

"Honestly?"

He nods.

"No, not really. My momma's death taught me that we should just live in the moment because tomorrow isn't promised. Do you ever think about it?"

"Sometimes. I mean, I wonder what it would be like to leave Grady," he replies.

He talks about leaving Grady a lot, but I never know serious he is.

I ask, "What do you think will happen with you and me? You think we'll always be close?"

"Hey," he says, getting my attention.

When I turn to look at him, he lays a hand on either side of my face, pulling me toward him until our lips touch.

I set one of my hands on top of his as he grabs my bottom lip between his. The way his soft lips feel against mine makes my stomach do flips.

When he finally pulls back, he looks into my eyes. "Sorry, I just had to know what it felt like to do that."

He looks so calm and relaxed. Meanwhile, I have to remind myself to breathe.

Grabbing my hand in his, he says, "Oh yeah, and to answer your question…yeah, I think we'll always be close."

"Oh yeah? Why's that?"

"Because I can't imagine not being able to do that every day."

# Chapter Eleven

## TRACY

"Trace. Trace...you doing okay?" My dad's voice pulls me out of my thoughts.

My head snaps toward him. "Yeah, I'm good—just a little tired. I'm sorry. What were you saying?"

His scruffy voice says, "Oh, nothing important. Just rambling. Why don't you tell me what's up with you? You seem like you're a million miles away."

"Really, it's nothing. Like I said, just a little tired."

"Does you being tired have anything to do with you sneaking off with Jessie Mitchell yesterday?"

My jaw drops open. "How on Earth did you hear about that?"

He chuckles. "I ran to the Stop 'N Go to pick up some coffee filters this morning. Brenda Jenkins asked me if I knew my daughter was *fornicating* with the town drug addict. Then, she went on to ask if you two get married, did I think that your kids would be drug addicts too."

My blood boils. "That nosey old cow! I'm going to kill her! What did you say?"

"I told her to mind her own business and that any questions she has about your love life should be directed to you."

I sigh. "For the record, Jessie and I didn't go into the woods to *fornicate*."

He shrugs. "I wouldn't care if you did."

"Really? Even after everything people are saying about Jessie? I'm a little surprised you're not going *protective father* on me."

His deep voice lets out a full-blown belly laugh. "Tracy, I'm under no delusions that you need me to protect you. You've been taking care of yourself for quite some time now. I trust you to make your own decisions without any input from me."

I pause for a moment. "What if I did ask for input from you? Hypothetically, I mean. What advice would you give me about Jessie Mitchell?"

"I always liked Jessie," he says.

"And?"

He leans back, folding his arms over his chest. "What are you looking for here, Trace? What's going on?"

"I don't know. I've been avoiding Jessie for months, and now that I'm not, it's bringing up all these old memories and feelings."

His forehead creases. "And that's a bad thing?"

"Maybe. What if it all blows up again?"

"What if it doesn't?"

"Are you advocating for this now?" I ask with a twinge of attitude.

"Tracy, you and that boy were together constantly from the time you were five years old. I couldn't pry you apart with a crowbar. I don't know what happened between the two of you, but I reckon it has to be pretty bad to make you stop talking."

"It was," I interrupt.

"But I also reckon that what the two of you had was special. Friendship...relationship...whatever it was... doesn't come around every day. Maybe something like that is worth trying to salvage."

"We were so young," I say, barely loud enough for him to hear.

"I was sixteen when I met your momma. And I knew from our first date that she was the one for me. Age doesn't mean shit when your gut is telling you it's right." He smiles at just the mention of my momma. Almost twenty years later, and he's still head-over-heels for her. Her death didn't change that. "Just promise me you won't cut off your feelings like you always do."

I return his smile as best I can. "I promise." Standing up, I stretch and point to the door. "I'm going to go out back and work on fixing that fence around the chicken coop."

Once I'm outside, I take a deep breath, inhaling the morning Tennessee air. It's another beautiful day in Grady.

While I work on the fence, I yawn at least ten times. When I got home last night, I barely slept a wink. My mind just raced with thoughts of Jessie. When we were in the bounce house, it took everything in me not to rip his clothes off and ride him. But I don't think that would make anything any easier.

But damn, does it sound like fun.

And then, I dreamed about our first kiss. That day changed everything.

Before that day, I never considered the future. I just rode through life by the seat of my pants. I think I always had a crush on Jessie, but if he hadn't made the first move, I probably wouldn't have. It's not because of anything like low self-esteem. I'd say it was more because I have a tendency to shove my feelings down and pretend they don't exist.

But the moment Jessie kissed me, all those feelings I'd been shoving down came flying back to the surface.

That day was when our relationship shifted from best friends to something much more. Although we still did all the things we used to do, we also started doing things like holding hands, cuddling, and making out every chance we got.

We were obsessed with each other. And when we added sex into the mix, we became even more infatuated. Of course, we were just a couple of kids who had no idea what we were doing, but we sure as hell had fun while we tried. I'm pretty sure I didn't know what a real orgasm was back then, but I have to say I've never felt the love that we shared in those moments ever since.

After that day, I'd think about what the future would

mean for Jessie and me.

Eventually, things got complicated, and we inevitably imploded. Until recently, I haven't imagined what things would be like had we not fallen apart.

But I sure am now. Well, more so, I'm thinking about what the future would hold for us if we decided to start something up again.

Over the years, I haven't been quite as wild as I used to be. Once I was out of high school, I worked three jobs to save up money. One of those jobs was working at Daisy's Boutique. Daisy was the owner—an older woman who had owned the store for years but was ready to retire. She asked me if I was interested in buying the store. She stayed on long enough for me to save up some money for a down payment, and she showed me the ropes of running a business. Shortly after I took over, she moved to Florida to be with her daughter.

Needless to say, getting to the point where I could own my own business before I turned 25 meant I had to get my shit together. No more getting into trouble.

I still like to go fishing or do pretty much anything else outside, but I don't do all the wild stuff I used to. Usually, I don't feel the need to.

Then, I get around Jessie Mitchell, and I want to crank up the radio and go joy-riding.

I'm not sure which is worse.

Having no fun at all...or having way too much.

# Chapter Twelve

## JESSIE

Shutting the door of my truck, I walk on the sidewalk heading toward the shop I'm looking for. I stop outside the door, glancing up at the sign.

**Daisy's Boutique.**

I've wanted to talk to Tracy since our bounce house fun, but I didn't have her number, and I didn't want to bother her yesterday when she was with her dad.

The door chimes as I walk through, and I hear Tracy from behind some boxes. "I'll be right there."

"Take your time," I reply, wondering if she recognizes it's me.

I look around at the walls that are painted purple with sparkly fabric draped everywhere. It's definitely geared more toward a younger female crowd.

There's a table with some folded shirts on it and a sign that reads:

*Welcome to Daisy's Boutique!*

*Thank you for choosing our store when there's so many to choose from. What makes Daisy's different? All of our clothing is made right here in the great state of Tennessee, and everything we sell is a hand-crafted item. What does that mean? All of our items come to us in small batches from local designers. Once they're all sold, we won't get that design again. That means you're getting a unique product that helps multiple small businesses in your area.*

*Not from around here? Check out our website any time to see what new inventory we have available. We can ship it to you!*

*Have any questions? Please don't hesitate to ask me! And thank you again!*

*-Tracy*

How does she do it?

Tracy finds a way to sell her solid business model while still making you feel like she's your oldest friend.

"Hi, how can I—" she pauses as soon as she sees me. "Help you?"

I point to a neon pink crop-top. "Yes, I was wondering if you have this in my size?"

"Depends." She smiles.

"On?"

"On whether or not you care if your nipples hang out the bottom."

I shake my head. "Not a problem. I actually have beautiful nipples."

She giggles. "Of course, you do. But really, Jess, what's up?"

"Well, I have a problem."

"Oh?"

I step closer to her. "Yeah. See, I really wanted to ask you to go on a date with me, but I realized I don't have your phone number. So, I decided to come here and kill two birds with one stone."

"A date?" She asks.

"Yes. You remember those things we used to go on? I pick you up and take you to dinner. You eat more food than what seems humanly possible. I drop you off and hope for a kiss at the end of the night. A date."

Her green eyes flick up to mine. "Let me ask you something first. Are you just asking me because of a lack of options?"

"What?" I ask.

"You said it yourself—you don't find a lot of girls to date. Are you asking me because there's no one else in this small town?"

I take another step toward her. Her back is now against the wall, and we're close enough that I can smell her coconut-scented shampoo.

"Now, you listen here, wild child," I begin. "I know better than to think Tracy Kennedy is a last resort. I'm asking because I miss you, and I'd like to take you out."

She thinks for a moment, and I can see her wheels turning. Then, finally, she says, "When?"

"Whenever you want. I work tonight, but then I'm off until Friday. You name the day."

"Tomorrow," she replies. "Seven o'clock."

She pulls a pen out from her back pocket and writes her number on my hand. "Text me, and I'll send you my address."

"Can't wait," I say.

"Yeah, well, get out of here before I change my mind." She gives me a smirk before walking off to get back to work.

Heading back toward my truck, I pull out my phone and plug in Tracy's number and shoot her a text so she has mine.

It's only a moment before a text comes through with her address, and another one comes through seconds later.

**See you tomorrow, wild child.**

# Chapter Thirteen

## TRACY

"Hello?" Andi answers the phone.

"Hey, what are you doing?" I ask.

"Not a lot. Jonas took the boys to his mom's for a while, so I should be cleaning, but I'm drinking wine instead."

"Want some company?"

"Another distraction? Hell yeah, come on over."

"Alright. I'm leaving the store now. See you soon."

I hang up the phone and head in that direction. Hopefully, Andi can give me some clarity.

Jessie Mitchell asked me on a date, and I can't decide how I feel about it. Okay, that's a lie. I'm excited about it—at least my heart is.

My head is weaving an entirely different web, so now, I need to figure out whether I should listen to it or tell it to shut the hell up.

*******************************************************

When I get to the Mitchell Ranch, Andi calls for me to come on in. When I do, I see she's standing at the fridge.

"Do you have any beer?" I ask, skipping any other greetings.

"Oh, it's been one of *those* days." She smiles. "And yes, Jonas Mitchell lives here. Of course, we have beer."

She takes one of the tall cans out and hands it to me before pouring herself another glass of wine. Once we each have a drink in our hands, she leads me out to the front porch. We each take a seat on a rocker, looking out over the front yard.

"So, what's wrong?" Andi asks.

"What do you mean?" I feign ignorance.

"Well, you never come over here after work unless you've got something on your mind. So, spill it. Does it have anything to do with your tryst with Jessie in the bounce house the other night?"

I choke on the sip of beer I just took. "You know about that?" She scoffs. "Of course, I know about that. Tracy, your laugh carries for miles. I had to turn up the TV on full volume, and Jonas still heard you guys. You're lucky I was able to wrangle him back inside."

I chuckle. "Thanks for that."

We both sip our drinks, and then, she says, "So, did you guys *do it?*"

Yet again, I'm choking on my beer. "What?! No, we didn't *do it!*"

She holds her hands up. "Just wondering. I mean, maybe it's time to dust the old girl off." She points a finger toward my crotch.

I use my hand to cover myself. "The old girl is just fine. Thank you."

"Well, what *is* going on with you and Jessie?"

"He asked me on a date."

She nods. "How should I react to that? Are you happy about it?"

I sigh. "I think so. But also terrified."

"Why? Because of his history with drugs and all that?"

I shake my head. "Nah, none of that bothers me. Everyone has their vices. I'm not going to judge him when he's trying to better himself."

"Then, what is it?" She asks.

"Back in the day, Jessie and I used to date."

Now, it's her turn to choke on her drink. "What?!"

"Well, I say we used to date, but that seems like too much of a generalization," I tell her the story of our friendship and how it turned into something more. I tell her about our exciting, crazy romance.

"What happened?" She asks when I finally come up for air.

I think for a moment before answering. "We had a fight—a big one. I let my temper get the best of me, and I called it off. When I calmed down and came to my senses, I went to apologize...but I found him in bed with a girl who lived in the next town over."

Her eyes go wide. "Did you kick both of their asses?"

I shake my head. "I never told him I saw. I just pushed him away and right on out of my life."

"I'm surprised."

"Why?"

"Because the Tracy Kennedy that I know would have kicked her ass and gave Jessie the tongue lashing of a lifetime." She snickers.

"Andi, I pushed him away. I broke up with him. I guess ultimately, he could fuck whoever he wanted."

She sets her hand on top of mine. "Doesn't mean that it hurts any less."

"Am I stupid for going on a date with him again...after all this time?"

"Do you still think about him or wonder what it may have been like if things had been different?"

"I didn't for years. I never let him even cross my mind."

Her eyes narrow. "And now?"

"Now, I can't think of anything *but* him."

"Then, maybe you should do it and see where it goes. What's the worst that can happen?"

"I don't know. That's what scares me."

# Chapter Fourteen

## JESSIE

Slowly, I pull my truck into the gravel driveway leading to Tracy's cute little house. Her home looks like it sits on a pretty decent-sized piece of land since none of her neighbors are too close. There's a house directly across the street, but that's the closest one for quite a while.

Part of me can't believe Tracy said yes to this date, so I've spent the past day and a half planning to make sure that it's one she'll never forget.

Before I can step out of the truck and get both feet on the ground, Tracy comes walking out her front door. And damn, she looks perfect.

Her hair is down and styled with its natural wave. Her face is natural except for a bit of sparkle on her eyelids.

My eyes travel further down, and I see that she's wearing a cute little sundress. It's yellow with tiny red flowers all over it —the yellow shows off her beautiful tan skin. The whole outfit is completed with some light-brown cowgirl boots.

As I get closer, she smiles at me. "Hey! Right on time."

I chuckle. "I may be an asshole at times, but I'm always a punctual one. Are you ready to go?"

She nods. "Whenever you are."

Walking back to the truck, I open the door for her, and she slides in.

Once I'm in on my side, I see her looking around at my old, beat-up vehicle.

"I know she doesn't look like much, but she's been a good truck so far."

"No judgment." She smiles. "My dad has had his practically my whole life. I love trucks. They seem to just keep running forever. Thought about getting one myself."

"Nothing sexier than a woman in a pick-up truck."

She just rolls her eyes at me and tries not to laugh.

We make some small talk about our days while we drive to the location I've picked out. It's an easy conversation, but it's as though something still hangs in the air between us.

A few minutes later, I pull the truck onto a dirt road that leads back to an old field. It hasn't been used for a while, and a couple of years ago, Jonas bought it and just hasn't done anything with it yet.

"Are you going to kill me and bury me out here?" She jokes.

"Not today," I say with a wink.

I keep my eyes on her face and watch it light up when she sees what I've done. In the middle of the empty field, I set up on the home movie projector with some string lights hanging around it. I back the truck up close to the screen, and she glances in the bed where I've laid some blankets and pillows.

"Assuming you might get lucky?" She asks, nodding to the bedding.

"Nope. Just wanted us to be comfortable. We can sit on the ground if you like."

She smiles. "The bed of the truck will be fine."

I walk over to help her out, but she's already gotten out by the time I get there.

When she sees what I was trying to do, she says, "Oh, sorry. Just a habit, I guess. Not used to anyone opening doors for me."

"We'll just have to change that, now won't we? I may have lived in the big city for a while, but I've never forgotten my manners."

"Your momma raised you right." She beams.

I beat her to the back of the truck and open the tailgate before helping her up into it. She gets comfortable while I grab the food I had stored in the backseat.

Climbing in after her, I take a seat and open the large bag. I stored it in one of those bags that keep things hot or cold.

"I spent a while trying to think of where to take you for dinner," I begin. "I didn't think fancy restaurants were Tracy Kennedy's style, but nothing in town seemed quite good enough. So, there's this cute little place I love not far from here, and I thought I'd get us—".

"Tacos," she interjects while inhaling deeply.

"How do you do that?" I ask, looking down. "I've barely even opened the bag."

She shrugs. "Full disclosure? I could smell them in the truck while they were zipped up in the bag."

"You're still a bloodhound, aren't you?" I ask, and her laughter fills the air between us.

Pulling some tacos out of the bag, I set them in front of us and grab a couple bottles of soda I had stored in a small cooler sitting in the corner.

"You've thought of everything, haven't you?" She asks.

"Tried to," I respond before we dig in.

The first bite touches her lips, and she moans. "Oh holy fuck, these are good."

"I know! It's just a little hole-in-the-wall place, but they make some amazing food. I haven't tried their margaritas, but I hear they're out of this world."

Her nose crinkles up. "Not really my thing. Give me a beer or some good whiskey, and I'm a happy girl."

I chuckle. "I'll keep that in mind for next time."

She starts stumbling over her words as she speaks. "Don't feel like you have to get me alcohol. I know you don't drink, and I don't want to make it hard for you."

Shaking my head, I reply, "T, I work in a bar. I'm used to being around people who are drinking. It won't bother me. Besides, it was never alcohol that I had a real issue with."

"So, why not drink if it was never an issue for you? I'm not judging. Just curious."

Before I answer, I finish the last bite of my taco. "I don't want to do anything that might cloud my senses. I don't want drinking to lead to something potentially worse."

"Fair enough. How long has it been?"

I know we've transitioned from talking about alcohol to the entirety of my bad habits.

"Over a year," I reply. "Look, T, I'm not saying it's easy because it's not, but for me, it isn't about missing the drugs. I mean, yeah, those were nice, but they were nice because they helped me forget all my problems. When I quit, all those things I was trying to forget came screaming back in full force. That was harder than any physical withdrawal symptom I went through."

Her hand rests on my knee as her fingers lightly rub the denim. "For what it's worth, I'm proud of you."

"Back at you, T."

"Why are you proud of me?" She looks confused.

"Look at you, T. You bought a house. You own your own business. You found a way to help your community with that business still. And you agreed to go out with me tonight even though I'm sure you had your reservations about it. You're just awesome, T."

"Thanks," she replies, barely looking at me. She still hates getting compliments.

"And I have to say that I'm a little surprised."

"Why?" She asks, opening another taco.

"I think these past few days, I've seen you in a dress more times than I have our entire lives."

She giggles. "You've only seen me in a dress twice the past few days."

"Exactly," I joke. "The Tracy Kennedy I knew back in the day *never* wore dresses."

She tucks her hair behind her ear. "I guess running the clothing store has made me expand my wardrobe a little. But don't get excited. I only wear them on special occasions."

I smile. "I'll just be thankful you consider this a special occasion."

We finish eating while we joke and catch up. Every moment I spend with her makes me realize even more how much I've missed her. She's the girl next door and the hell-raiser all rolled into one.

Once we've finished eating, I gather up all the trash and put it in the backseat. I hand Tracy a few movies to pick from, and she chooses the most action-packed one.

*No surprise there. She never cared for chick-flicks.*

Before she hands them back, she says, "This is a really sweet idea, Jess. What made you think of it?"

"I remembered when we were kids, and you and I would always have to travel so far to go see a movie. Half the time, we wouldn't end up going. So, I figured I'd bring the movie theatre to us."

"That's sweet," she says with a smile. But she looks like the cat who ate the canary.

"What?" I ask.

Sheepishly, she replies, "They built a movie theatre over in Rogersburg."

Rogersburg is the next town over. A twenty-minute drive, tops.

"Well, shit. I had no idea. I'm sorry. I should've—"

She cuts me off. "No. This is way better. Really."

And I believe her. I smile at her and hop down to start the movie on the projector.

When I come back, Tracy is sitting propped up against the truck's cab with a few pillows behind her back. I start to crawl to get into position next to her.

Without warning, her fingers wrap around the collar of my shirt as she pulls me toward her. When she tugs me close, our mouths meet. Her lips press firmly against mine, and I run my tongue across the seam of her mouth. She opens, and our tongues dance.

When she pulls back, she looks up at me and smiles. "Sorry, I just wanted to know what that would feel like."

We both grin, and I get comfortable next to her, wrapping my arm around her shoulders.

The movie starts to play, but I know I'm not going to be able to concentrate.

Not after that fucking kiss.

# Chapter Fifteen

## TRACY

Those butterflies that have been in my stomach all day turned into bats that moment my lips touched Jessie's. All those years ago, when he kissed me, something shifted. This time though, it's like something shifted back.

His lips against mine brought back a sense of familiarity. All those feelings came back, and I felt…home.

Now, we are cuddled up watching the movie. Playfully, I take Jessie's hat off his head and put it on my own.

"I love a woman in a baseball cap," he says with a sexy grin.

Part-way into the movie, he pulls out some boxes of candy and a bag of popcorn.

"You really did think of everything," I say.

"Well, we can't go to the movies without snacks, now can we, beautiful?"

We eat and talk, only half paying attention to the movie. I'm surprised when he doesn't try to kiss me again, but I'm guessing he wants to respect any boundaries I may have.

We watch the sunset in all of its beautiful glory, and when the air starts to cool, we cuddle under the blanket.

It reminds me of our younger years, except now, some-how, it feels more real…as crazy as that sounds.

When the movie is over, we pack up the truck and head back toward my house. He holds my hand on the drive, stroking my fingers with his thumb. It's such a simple gesture yet still makes me feel all warm and tingly.

*Good lord, I sound like such a girl.*

When he stops the truck, I decide to stay inside and wait until he comes around to open my door for me. I'm not used to it, but the gesture is nice. Chivalry is a big deal around here.

The door opens, and he holds out his hand for mine. Even after he helps me down, our fingers stay intertwined.

It's nice.

He walks me to my door, and we stop on the porch.

"Tonight was—" I begin.

"Not what you were expecting?" He interrupts.

"Perfect," I finish. "Tonight was perfect. All these years later, you still know the way to my heart."

He smiles. "Yep. Directly through your stomach."

A loud laugh escapes me. "Exactly."

As unsure as I was about this whole date, I couldn't be happier that I said yes. Jessie is just as sweet as I remember. And somehow, this evening, none of the bad stuff seems to matter.

"Can I take you out again?" He asks.

I nod and lean up on my tiptoes to kiss him. It's soft and easy, but I crave more.

My head is swirling with a thousand thoughts, and I know I'm not thinking clearly, but I don't care.

I watch Jessie walk back toward his truck, and without overthinking it, I call out his name.

When he turns around, my feet take off toward him, and I jump into his arms, wrapping my legs around his waist.

My arms hook around his neck as I pull him close, my mouth finding his once more. His tongue seeks entrance, and I immediately give it to him. He swoops in, and I love the taste of him.

Every kiss sends heat straight to my core. One of his hands holds firmly onto my ass, while the other holds my face while we continue our heated make-out session.

When I finally come up for air, I whisper, "Let's go inside. I have nosy neighbors."

"We don't have to if you don't want to."

My tongue flicks out to lick along his bottom lip. "Take me inside," I say once more.

This time, he doesn't argue. He doesn't say a word as he heads towards the front door. Once there, I pull out my keys to unlock it, all while still in Jessie's arms.

Once we're through the door, he kicks it closed with his foot. It takes less than a second before his mouth is back on mine. He backs me up, so my body is trapped between him and the wall.

The friction from the denim of his jeans rubbing against my panties makes me let out a soft moan.

He grabs my arms from around his neck and pins them above my head against the wall. Holding them in place, he trails kisses along my jawline and then down to my neck and chest.

"God, I've missed you," he whispers against my skin.

It feels so good I can barely get out, "I missed you too."

His teeth gently nip at my earlobe as he transitions into holding up both of my hands with just one of his. His other hand moves to my breast, where his thumb grazes my nipple through the thin fabric of the dress.

At this moment, I'm grateful for my smaller chest. Not having to wear a bra means less material between us.

"Bedroom," I moan.

As if running on instinct alone, he carries me in the direction of my room. While he walks, it's my turn to kiss his neck and tease him just a little.

Once we are through the door, he sets me down on the bed. Before he can stand back up, I immediately pull him back down on top of me.

His hard, lean body feels so good on top of mine. My fingers grasp the hem of his t-shirt and pull it over his head. My eyes gaze at his chest and stomach. They're hard but not overly defined, and his chest has a little bit of hair on it that leads down to a trail which goes *all* the way down, disappearing beneath his jeans. His jeans, which are doing nothing to hide the bulge of his hard cock.

My fingers undo the button on them, and my hand reaches into his boxers, feeling his hard length beneath my fingers. I pull it out and stroke the soft skin. It's long and thin and stands straight up, pointing at his stomach. It's bigger than I remember when we used to do this.

Leaning me back, he yanks the straps of my dress off my shoulders and drags the entire thing down my body until it slides off my feet.

"Holy shit, baby girl," he says, taking a look at me before his mouth finds one of my small, pebbled nipples. He flicks his tongue back and forth over it, and I run my fingers through his hair, gently tugging. Every flick of his tongue makes my clit throb with need.

After focusing on my other nipple for a moment, his head moves further down until it's planted between my legs.

Breathless, I moan, "As much as I want you to do that, right now, I *really* need you inside me. Fuck me, Jessie."

"Baby girl, you keep talking like that, this will be over before we even get started."

While he finishes pulling his pants off, I give him a wicked smile. "Then, I guess we would just have to do it again."

"God, you're perfect."

He yanks my panties down so hard I'm pretty sure they rip. Then, with just one finger, he glides through my slit, making sure I'm wet enough for him. When his finger touches my clit, my hips arch upward, begging for more contact on the sensitive nub. But instead of giving it to me, he pulls his hand away and licks his finger.

I don't know what about that is so sexy, but damnit, it is.

As if coming to a sudden realization, he mutters something about a condom. But I don't want to wait. I've been on the pill for years and never had a pregnancy scare. When I whisper to him that we don't need a condom, he grins.

Without wasting another moment, he lines up with my

entrance and pushes inside. The moment he slides across my threshold, my back arches toward him.

He starts slow until I get used to his size. Once he's fully inside, I moan, "Harder, Jessie."

Obeying my command, he quickens his pace and slams into me. My pussy is more and more electrified with every thrust.

I pull him down for a kiss while my tongue slips into his mouth. My legs wrap around his back, holding him in place while he brings me closer to the edge.

Sweat breaks out over both of our bodies as we get lost in the moment. All I feel is my body coming to life for him. All I hear are our heavy breaths and our bodies slapping together. And all I can see is him…Jessie Mitchell—the man who is slowly stealing my heart once again.

The man I tried so hard to forget.

But now, I wonder how he'll ever leave my mind for even a moment from now on.

He sits up on his knees and spreads my legs even wider. His hand disappears between us, and I feel his fingers start rubbing my clit in smalls circles. As he speeds up his tempo with his cock, his fingers work faster too.

"Oh yeah. Right there," I moan.

"That's it, baby girl. Come for me. I want to see it."

His dirty talk is just enough to push me over the edge. Heat starts in my core and spreads all throughout my veins.

My body quakes beneath him as he keeps thrusting until finding his own release. He groans as he finishes, and then he leans down and kisses me once more.

When he finally pulls out of me, he goes to the bathroom to grab and towel and then takes the time to clean me up.

"You don't have to do that, you know?" I ask.

"Baby girl, you just let me into that sweet pussy of yours. The least I can do is clean up my mess."

Once he's done, he tosses the towel into the hamper and climbs into bed next to me. Then, scooting closer, he wraps his arms around my waist and kisses me once more—softly, sensually.

When he pulls back, he's got the biggest grin on his face.

"What?" I ask.

"I just can't believe I'm here with you, like this. But I guess I should've known better," he says, twirling a strand of my hair around his finger.

"Known what?"

"That the moment I was around you, I would fall for you all over again."

I can't help but smile. "Anyone ever tell you you're a real smooth talker?"

"Oh yeah, this spit-fire country girl who loves to bust my balls for it."

"I bet she's lovely," I joke.

"Oh, she is. But she's also a huge pain in my ass." He winks. "See, I think she doesn't like my smooth-talking because she thinks I'm just feeding her some bullshit."

"And you're not?"

He shakes his head. "Not in the least. I've missed her something fierce, and I think she should know that."

He leans in for another kiss, and I can feel the smile still on his lips.

I know we still have so much to talk about—so much to work through. But this moment is too perfect to fuck up. I just want it to go on a little bit longer.

Pulling him closer, I deepen the kiss. Our tongues explore each other, and I love how he tastes.

I let out a slight giggle, and he leans back to look at me.

I say, "Just thinking about how I'm really glad you didn't smoke before tonight."

"If I get to do this every day, I'll never smoke another cigarette again," he growls before starting our kiss once more.

We lie there making out for what feels like hours. Jessie eventually starts to move between my legs to get back on top of me, but I gently push him onto his back and climb on top of him instead.

Straddling him, I whisper, "My turn."

# Chapter Sixteen

## JESSIE

*Holy shit, this woman is a goddess. Even more perfect than what I remember.*

She climbs on top of me and aligns herself with the tip of my dick, slowly sinking down on it. Now, she's grinding against me as she moves her hips up and down.

Tracy has always been a firecracker in bed, but she's even more enthusiastic now.

*My God, the woman can ride a dick.*

She leans down to kiss me while decreasing her tempo to be teasingly slow.

My hands each grab a fistful of her round ass. She moans as I give it a soft smack. Seeing she likes it, I give her a couple more.

I can tell she's getting closer because her moans are getting louder. Gently, I push on her shoulders.

"Sit up," I command. "Let me see you, baby girl."

Once she's sitting up, I add, "Fucking beautiful."

"Jessie," she moans my name. "Fuck, yes."

If she keeps moaning my name like that, I'm going to fucking blow.

My eyes rake over her body and take in how sexy she is. Her soft, petite body feels so good under my fingertips. And her pussy is squeezing me like a fist.

She reaches up and rolls her nipples between her fingers. Watching the way she likes it done, I replace her hands with my own.

"Mine," I whisper.

Her nails dig into my chest as she braces to ride me harder. The faster she goes, the louder she gets, and it's the hottest thing I've ever seen.

I've been with my fair share of women. Back in Nashville, before I got serious with Gabby, I had some good sex with some beautiful women. But none of them even come close to Tracy.

The woman fucks just like she lives her life...to the absolute fullest. When we were younger, she was the same way, but now, there's a new confidence in her. It's like she knows exactly what she wants and isn't afraid to take it.

I feel her clench around me as she finds her release.

"Yeah, T. That's it, baby girl," I say while she comes.

She screams as her body quakes on top of me. She's so tight around my dick that I follow her right over the edge.

Once her body stills, I pull her down for a kiss before she collapses on the bed next to me.

"Damn, we are way better at that now than we used to be," she giggles, out of breath. "And think of all those years we missed out on."

"Yeah, but there *is* an upside to that, you know?" I ask.

"What's that?"

I smile. "We get to have a whole hell of a lot of fun making up for lost time."

# Chapter Seventeen

## TRACY

The next morning, my alarm goes off way too early. I shut it off, and as I attempt to roll out of bed, I feel an arm pull me back down.

"Don't go," Jessie whispers against the back of my neck. His breath makes goosebumps erupt all over my skin.

"I have to. All the girls I have on the schedule at the store today don't come in until this afternoon. That means it's just me this morning," I say. "And if the store's not open, I can't make any money."

He kisses the back of my shoulder. "I'll buy twenty of those tight pairs of jeans if you stay here."

I chuckle. "You're not really my key demographic. Besides —" I reach around and grab his half-hard dick. "I don't think *this* would fit in those tight jeans."

I give it a final squeeze before getting out of bed.

"Oh, that's just mean," he sighs, reaching his arm out again but this time finding an empty space.

I lean down to kiss his cheek. "How about I make it up to you tonight?" I ask.

"Tonight? Sounds good."

"You want to hang at your place? I'll bring dinner."

He nods. "Sure. Although I must say that my place isn't nearly as homey as yours."

I look around. "Mine isn't all that. Just my home base. A place to lay my head down at night."

His thumb strokes my cheek. "But it's *yours,* and that's something to be damn proud of. You should be proud of your home and your business."

"That's nice to hear. My date the other night told me that running a business is a man's job and that I'll eventually have to sell the business to stay home and have babies."

He scoffs. "Bullshit. Nobody says you can't have it all, and for the record, you won't be going on any more bad dates for a long, long time."

"Is that so?"

"I mean, you could, but then, I'd tag along, and it might just get awkward." He winks.

I just smile and shake my head as I stand back up. "Do you want to hop in the shower with me?"

"Baby girl, as much as I would love that, if I go in there with you, you'll never make it to work on time." He gets up and pulls his jeans back on. I'm a little disappointed when his shirt follows. I really like staring at him naked.

Walking over to me, he sets a hand on each side of my face and kisses me. It's slow and seductive, and I don't want it to end.

But it does. And when he pulls away, I instantly miss the contact.

"I'll see you tonight, beautiful," he says with a grin before heading out the front door.

And I watch his ass the entire time as he walks away.

Once I hear him leave, I get in the shower. The whole time, thinking of nothing but Jessie Mitchell.

*******************************************************************

It's early afternoon, and my ass is seriously dragging at this point. As much fun as my sexy time with Jessie was last night, it didn't allow much time for sleep. And I *really* enjoy my sleep.

I'm running full speed all day long, so I need sleep to recharge my batteries.

But damn, the lack of sleep was worth it. Sex with Jessie was...amazing. It might sound cliche, but the man still knows how to read my body.

And now, he's even better at it.

I'm not sure exactly what came over me when I jumped into his arms and kissed him. But the moment I did, everything seemed just to click.

There were no mad memories. No painful past. No awkward moments.

Just us.

And all the feelings we've always had for one another.

I'm so entirely trapped inside my own head, replaying the events of the night that I about jump out of my skin when the door to the store chimes.

Peeking around the display I've been working on, I see a mess of springy black curls, and I immediately know it's Andi.

"Hey, you," I greet, walking toward her.

"What's up, buttercup?" She smiles. "I brought you something."

She hands me a travel mug full of coffee.

Taking it from her, I slip open the top and inhale deeply. "You're a saint," I groan before taking the first sip.

"Good?" She asks.

I just give a guttural moan in response.

"Figured you might need some caffeine...after your late night last night," she says, sipping from her own mug.

Slowly, I pull the drink from my mouth. "What do you know?"

"Oh, nothing..."

My eyes roll. "Spill it, Andi."

"Well, Jonas happened to notice that his brother never came home last night. And this morning, I took the boys to school, and Marlow Woodard practically waved me down to ask me if I knew why Jessie Mitchell was at her neighbor's house all night."

"I'm getting really tired of that old bitty sticking her nose into my business," I sigh.

"So, are you going to tell me about your night?" She asks. "How was the date?"

"Damn near perfect."

"And how was the..." She wiggles her eyebrows up and down.

"That was pretty perfect too." I smile and lead her back to my office, where we can sit down. "The man knows what he's doing in that department."

She giggles. "Must be something about those Mitchell boys. It's like someone gave them a handbook or something."

"Or they've just had a lot of practice," I quip.

Her nose scrunches up. "I choose to ignore that notion. The man might have a past, but I don't need to know about it."

"You know Jonas was engaged to Nicole?"

"Well, yeah, everyone in this town made sure I knew that. But I like Nicole, so I pretend that never happened either." She laughs. "Speaking of pasts, did you and Jessie talk about your guys' past?"

I take another sip. "Not yet."

"You planning on it?"

"Yes, Mom," I say with a sarcastic sigh.

"Trace, I'm not trying to bust your balls, but two days ago, you were so worried about history repeating itself. So, I figured you would have discussed it."

I nod. "I know. Everything was so perfect. I didn't want to ruin it. But I'm seeing him tonight, so we can talk about it then."

"Okay. Just trust me when I say it's so much easier after you have the dreaded conversation. Then, nothing will be holding you back."

I start laughing, and she looks confused.

Still giggling, I answer, "I just remember not too long ago when I was the one giving you dating advice. Now, you're married and a mom."

"Guess it was pretty good advice, huh?" She grins.

"Guess so."

Our chit-chat is interrupted when the door chimes with an incoming customer. Andi tells me to call her later and heads out, so I can get back to work.

I spend the next hour helping a mom pick out some birthday gifts for her daughter. But my mind still occasionally drifts back to Jessie.

Andi's right. We need to talk about the past to be able to move on to the future...*if* there's a future.

Tonight, we will have that conversation.

# Chapter Eighteen

## JESSIE

When I left Tracy's, I probably should have gone home and gone back to sleep, but I was too wired. The girl of my dreams was finally back in my arms. Who could sleep after that?

Instead, I went for a run around the ranch. My feet instinctively led me back to the lake, but I didn't stay long. It just didn't feel the same without Tracy.

When I got tired of running, I came across Taylor, Jonas's second in command on the ranch. He was moving some hay bales, so I decided to stop and help.

Pretty much, I spent my entire day trying to keep busy, biding time until this evening. My boredom makes me think I need to get some new hobbies. Typically, I only work at the bar on weekends, so my weekdays tend to drag on—even more so when I have plans with a beautiful woman to look forward to.

I straighten up the house as best I can. I'm not overly messy, but I'm not a good deep-cleaner either. I try to keep it halfway decent, though, because most of the stuff in here isn't mine.

When Andi first moved to Grady, she was living here. When she and Jonas got together, she moved in with him and left most of her furniture here. So, I didn't have to buy much, which was good because I left Nashville with nothing but the clothes on my back and the money in my wallet.

I'm just getting out of the shower when I hear a knock on the door. Quickly, I pull on my jeans and jog to answer it.

Holding a pizza, Tracy smiles when she sees me.

"Hey, T," I return her grin.

"Hi." She glances at the box. "I brought dinner."

"Thank goodness. I'm starving." I step out of the way so she can come inside.

As soon as she sets the pizza down on the coffee table, I spin her around, so she's facing me. Grabbing her face, I bring my lips to hers. She melts into my kiss, and it feels so dang good.

When I finally break it, her tongue licks her bottom lip before saying, "If you keep that up, our pizza will get cold."

"I like cold pizza," I whisper as my tongue mimics hers in tracing her bottom lip.

"Then, what are you waiting for?" She asks.

Her little taunt is all it takes to make me lose control. Not wanting to waste time going to the bedroom, I stay right in front of the couch.

"Take off your pants," I command.

She does so, and I remove mine.

Next, I pull off her tank top and about lose my mind seeing her with no bra.

Laying her down, I run a finger through her folds to make sure she's ready.

"So wet, baby girl," I groan before replacing my fingers with my cock.

She cries out as I sink myself into her warmth. I begin to move, and she encourages me to go harder and faster. I do as she asks and give it to her just like she wants it.

This will be a sprint more than a marathon, but I'm going to make sure she crosses the finish line.

I set her legs on my shoulders, angling her, so I'm making perfect contact with her G-spot. She reaches down and rubs her clit as her body writhes beneath me.

It doesn't take long at all before I feel her coming on my

dick, her pussy pulsing around me.

Once she's satisfied, I let go and give her my own release. I give her a quick kiss before going to get a towel to clean her up.

"Do you have a t-shirt I can wear?" She calls after me.

*Fuck yes, I do. It's sexy as hell to see a woman in my shirt.*

I bring her out a clean t-shirt and hand it to her while I take my time cleaning her up. Once I'm done, I grab a couple of plates and bottles of water, and we dig in.

The pizza's a little cold but not too bad.

"How was your day?" She asks between bites.

"Pretty damn boring," I respond. "Tell me about yours."

She shrugs. "It was alright. I got a couple of new shipments in, so I was getting them all tagged and stocked. Nicole is coming in tomorrow to model them so I can take pictures for the website."

I take another bite. "Why don't *you* model the clothes?"

She throws her head back and laughs. "Have you seen Nicole? And have you seen me?"

"I don't see your point."

She wipes her mouth with a paper towel. "Nicole is like a freaking goddess with her long legs and perfectly proportioned body. I'm sure people would rather stare at her with her flawless skin and long blonde hair. She looks amazing in anything."

"Let me ask you something, T. How many women do you know with Nicole's proportions?"

She shrugs. "Not a lot."

"Exactly. Why wouldn't you want to put more relatable women on there? And for the record, not everyone wants to look at Nicole. I'd rather look at you."

Her eyes roll. "You're a little bias because you get to see me naked."

"True." I laugh. "But I think you'd look just as good in any of that stuff as she would. Promise me you'll at least think of modeling some of it for your site."

She's quiet for a moment. "I'll think about it."

I grin at the small victory because they're hard to come by

with a woman like Tracy Kennedy.

We finish eating our pizza while we talk and laugh. It feels just like it did when we were young.

No, scratch that.

It's better.

Back then, I was an idiot. Although I was crazy about Tracy, I was so anxious to get out of Grady that I was too blind to see what was right in front of my face. It was like I expected Tracy to give up what she wanted and follow me to the ends of the Earth.

Damn, I'm glad she didn't. Not following that dumb ol' boy meant she built a wonderful life for herself.

And I make a mental promise to myself that I'm not going to bring down her life in any way now that I'm back in it.

But that promise is about to be put to the test.

When Tracy sets her water bottle down on the end table, it tips over, spilling a little bit.

Quickly, I stand up to grab some paper towels to clean it up, but she takes them from me.

"Shit. I'm sorry," she says, wiping up the mess.

"No big deal, baby girl. It's just water."

She goes to move the small wooden box that holds all my secrets. She wipes underneath it, and it falls from her hand and hits the couch.

Out falls the grainy black and white photo I stare at every night.

She murmurs a curse word at her clumsiness before kneeling to pick it up. When her eyes lock on what it is, they go wide.

"Hey Jessie," she begins, and I brace for impact. "I think it's time you tell me what happened in Nashville."

# Chapter Nineteen

## TRACY

**M**y eyes keep staring at the tiny sonogram photo in my hand, and my mind races with questions.

*Does Jessie have a kid out there?*

*Did he leave that kid?*

*What the hell happened?*

"You may want to get comfortable. It's a long story," he says.

I set the photo on the coffee table, lying face down, so I'm not staring at it the whole time. I don't utter a word, instead just waiting for him to begin.

"I'm sure you know that the second half of our senior year, I started hanging out with the wrong crowd. We were drinking all the time. Partying. Smoking weed. Once we graduated, we decided to go to Nashville because there was a talk of some job opportunities in construction. But once we got there, the bright city lights suckered us in. Every night was a different bar and a different woman in our beds."

He must notice my slight flinch at the mention of his playboy lifestyle because he says, "Sorry. Just trying to be honest."

"Jessie, I wasn't a monk while you were gone. I did fuck people too. I'm fine. Go on."

He nods. "Fair enough. Eventually, our smoking weed turned into doing pills and lines of cocaine. The rush was incredible, but the crash sucked. So, we tended to stay high most of the time. Coke to get going and pills to sleep. When money started to dry up, we came back to town for a couple of days. I asked Jonas for a loan, and he told me no. After tearing apart his house and not finding anything, I went to Momma's and took all the cash she had saved up. Honestly, I remember doing it, but when I think about it, it's like I'm watching someone else do it. Like a movie or something. I can't believe I did that to her."

The last words are spoken softly, and he chokes on them while wiping a small tear from the corner of his eye.

I scoot closer to him and gently rub his arm before interlocking my fingers with his. I can tell how hard this is for him, and I want him to know he's not alone.

He pauses for a moment to give me a small smile. "Once we blew through that money, we all got jobs at a bar. It was another way to keep us drinking and partying while meeting easy women."

"One night, a cute girl named Gabby walked in. She was more of a partier than I was, and she sucked me right into her world. Her parents were pretty well-off, and she was a trust fund kid. So, she made sure we were always taken care of, so to speak."

He looks down at his hands and avoids my eyes. "Things started to get worse. We were losing entire chunks of time, and I couldn't think straight. Needless to say, we didn't have the wherewithal always to use a condom, and she ended up pregnant."

I squeeze his hand tighter as I brace for impact. "The moment that test turned positive, my mental fog lifted. I'd never been so clear in all my life. After that, I stopped drinking, stopped the drugs, stopped partying."

"We didn't find out she was pregnant until later than people usually do, so we were both terrified something was wrong. But when we went to the doctor, they ran a ton of tests on the baby and us, and our little boy was perfect.

"When we got home, we made a promise to stop our partying lifestyle. We would do better for our baby. So, the next day, I went and got a second job. Gabby didn't want to work, and I didn't want her to have any stress."

He runs his hand through his hair and sighs. "I was working all the time and bringing home as much money as I could. The problem was that Gabby didn't like being alone just as much as she didn't like working. And being lonely wasn't good for her recovery.

"I came home from working at the bar one night and found her passed out cold on the bathroom floor. She'd taken a cocktail of who even knows what. I called an ambulance, and by the time they brought her back from the brink, we'd lost our baby.

"I was furious and devastated at the same time. Gabby begged and pleaded with me not to leave. She promised me that she would change and that she was sorry. She told me she wanted us to try again for a baby. We'd do it right this time around. I kept working, and we started trying but had no luck. When I found the new pack of birth control she'd been taking, of course, I was confused. When I went to confront her about it, I found her high-as-hell blowing her dealer. So, I left. I didn't even take the time to pack a bag. Just left everything behind to run home with my tail between my legs."

*Holy shit, that's a lot of information to take in.*

I knew Jessie had some trouble in the past, but I had no idea things got as bad as they did.

"Jessie," I begin, but he puts his hand up.

"T, I didn't tell you all that for sympathy. The whole situation is an awful one, but I feel like I brought a lot of it on myself. I'm telling you this, so you don't think I'm keeping any secrets. Because truth be told, I'm crazy about you. And I don't want to lose you because my past comes back to haunt us. I promise you that I'm doing my best to lead a better life, and I look at that photo every night to remind me of what I'm working toward."

There are a million things I want to say to him about how I don't blame him for his past. And how proud I am of all the progress he's made. And how sorry I am for everything he had to go through.

But somehow, nothing I say will sound like nearly enough. So instead, I crawl into his lap so that I'm straddling him. Wrapping my arms around his neck, I pull him close and kiss him softly—first on his lips and then peppering kisses all over the rest of his face.

When I find his lips again, we spend a few moments just kissing. It's not sexual. It's not leading anywhere. It's a sweet kiss filled with all of the things I want to say to him. He lays his hands on my hips, and I can feel his entire body relax.

When we pull away, I stand up and reach for his hand.

"Let's go to bed," I say.

He takes my hand and stands up to follow me. Once we are cuddled up in his bed, I get comfortable in his arms. They make me feel safe, and that's saying a lot for a girl who doesn't ever *need* anyone.

My head rests on his chest, and I slowly begin to drift off, listening to the melodic rhythm of his heart.

Tonight, he opened up to me and bared his soul. Although we still haven't talked about our own sordid past, it feels like we took a step in the right direction.

And for now, that's enough.

# Chapter Twenty

### JESSIE

The next evening, I'm whipping up some dinner for Tracy and myself as I wait for her to arrive. Earlier, she texted me saying she was having a shitty day and was in a bad mood. She tried to cancel our plans for tonight due to her foul mood, but I convinced her to come over, and I'd make dinner.

So, I ran to the Stop 'N Go and got a couple of steaks and baked potatoes. I even picked up a six-pack of beer for her, which got me some dirty looks from everyone I came across. I probably should have just grabbed some from Jonas.

My plan is to feed Tracy a good meal, give her a shit-ton of orgasms, and make her forget all about her bad day.

I'm almost finished cooking when I hear a knock on the door.

"Come in," I call as I grab the potatoes out of the oven.

"Hey, baby girl," I greet as she comes into view.

"Hey, sweets," she says with a weak smile. "Something smells amazing."

"Steak and potatoes," I reply.

"Mmmm. Sounds delicious."

As quickly as I can, I plate everything and set it on the table. When I put a beer in front of her, her eyes go wide, and she chuckles.

"That explains why I had a few people stop by the store

today and apologize."

"Huh?"

"Oh, apparently, word of you buying beer spread like wildfire around town, and a couple of the gossips came in to tell me how sorry they were that you fell off the wagon."

"Shit, T. I'm sorry. I didn't mean to do anything to bother you at work. I just knew you said you were having a shitty day, and I was trying to make it better."

She shakes her head. "Don't worry about it. I told them to fuck off and mind their business. I don't let those busy-bodies ruin my day."

"So, do you want to talk about what *did* ruin your day?"

She lets out a loud sigh. "My dad and I got into it this morning because he tried doing too much and hurt his back… again. Then, I learned there's someone online trying to copy all our unique designs at the store and sell them as their own. And then, I had a rude customer yell at me because we didn't have her size in one of the discontinued clearance items. I offered to let her pick out something else for the same price, but she just wanted to argue."

"I'm sorry, baby girl."

"It's fine. Some days are just worse than others. It happens." Her words are sure, but her tone? Not so much.

Once we finish eating, we move over to the couch. Taking her legs in my lap, I take off her boots and start to rub her feet.

She lets out a soft moan while sipping her beer.

She holds up the bottle. "You didn't have to get this for me. I'm okay with not drinking when we are spending time together."

"Baby girl, I've already told you that your drinking doesn't bother me. And even if it did, I'd get over it. I'd like us to spend a whole lot of time together, and I'm not going to let some alcohol get in the way of that."

She flashes me a warm smile.

I continue, "But I did want to talk to you about something. Last night, I dumped a whole lot of baggage on you, and you were so amazing about all of it. Today, I realized that I didn't ask you if you had any questions or anything. So, if there's anything you want to know, ask away. I'm an open book."

She thinks for a minute, starting to pick at the label on her bottle. I can see the wheels turning. Finally, she says, "Did you love Gabby?"

I think about my answer before I speak, although I really don't need to. "I thought I did. But I realized it was more infatuation. She helped me forget every problem I had...until she started being the cause of my problems. And when I caught her sucking another guy's dick, I thought I'd be more upset than I was. I realized maybe she never cared about me if she was able to do that so easily."

Tracy's face suddenly falls. "Is that how you feel? If you do something like that with someone else, you're not really in love?" She pointedly asks.

"I don't know. But considering the kind of person Gabby was, I have other reasons for doubting she loved me."

Without looking at me, she stands up. "I should go," she announces.

"What?! Why?!"

She pulls on her boots and begins to head toward the door. Standing up, I walk after her, grabbing her and gently turning her around. When she faces me, I can see tears are gleaming in her eyes.

"Tracy, tell me what's wrong," I plead.

"You really have no idea what happened back then, do you?" She asks.

My mind struggles to keep up with her. "When? In high school? I remember we had a big fight, and you walked away."

She cuts me off. "Yeah, and then I came to apologize, and I saw you in bed with Sheila Evans."

Her words hit me like a smack across the face. I had no idea she saw that, and it was, and still is, one of my biggest regrets. But everything is starting to make a lot more sense.

"T, I had no idea."

"I know. We had that big fight about you moving away, and a few days later, I came to apologize and tell you I'd come with you. But, then, I saw you." Tears are now falling freely from her eyes.

She turns to walk away again, but I stop her once more. "Hold up a minute. I think you're forgetting an essential part of this story. I came to tell you about that. Remember that party in the cornfield we all went to? I came to tell you everything. I came to beg for your forgiveness. But you wouldn't do so much as look at me. I told you I was in love with you, and you walked away."

"Of course, I walked away," she cries. "I was devastated."

"I'm not saying I didn't fuck up. I did. When I thought you were done, I got drunk, and Sheila was just there. Even while we were doing it, I knew it wasn't right. I couldn't even finish because I couldn't stop seeing your face. But I don't blame you for walking away. I know how hard it must have been to see that."

We're both quiet for a moment while I rake my fingers through my hair. "Man, we really messed everything up back then, didn't we?"

"Sex makes everything all cloudy. It did back then, and it is now. I can't do this."

She heads toward the door once more, and I watch my future about to go up in smoke.

I'll be damned if I let that happen.

# Chapter Twenty-one

## TRACY

Jessie's hand reaches over me and shuts the door, stopping me from leaving. I reach up and wipe a tear off my cheek. I haven't cried like this in years, and I swear every pent up emotion I have is leaking through my eyes.

He leans forward and whispers in my ear, "Why do you think sex is clouding things up now?"

My lip quivers as I speak. "Look at us! We're already fighting."

I didn't come here ready to have this talk tonight. I came here to forget about my shitty day. My mood told me I shouldn't have started any type of serious conversation, but when Jessie mentioned the thing about Gabby never really loving him, the dam broke.

Still talking low in my ear, Jessie says, "Yeah, you know why we are fighting? Because we should have had this fight seven years ago. But we never did. I'd say it's about time we had it out, don't you?"

"Do you really think this is a good way to start a relationship?" I ask.

He turns me around, so I'm facing him with my back against the wall. "I think you're mistaken on something. This isn't the *start* of a relationship. You and I have been doing this for a long time now. This is you and I coming back from some stupid teenage mistakes. You want to know what's different between now and then, though?" He leans in even closer and whispers, "I'm not going to let you go without a fight this time around. I'm going to do whatever it takes to keep you by my side."

"But—" I begin

"No buts. Tracy Kennedy, I'm in love with you. I was pretty sure I was in love with you when you saved my ass in Kindergarten. And I *knew* I was in love with you the first time I kissed you. And I sure as hell am still sure of it now. Is it going to be rough sometimes? Sure. You're dating the town fuck-up. But I swear to you that no one will ever love you more. And I'll never stop fighting for us. And I'm sorry I let you go for so long." Emotion makes him choke on the last words.

"Tracy, I have a fucked up past, and being with me may not always be easy. But I promise I'll do my best to make you happy. You know how I told you I look at that photo every night because it gives me a reason to stay clean?"

I nod.

"Well, since you came back into my life, I have another reason."

I look into his blue eyes to look for any sign that he's feeding me a load of bullshit, but I find none. Through it all, though, these past few days with Jessie have been some of the best I've had in a long time. I can't deny that fact.

For a woman who preaches about living life to the fullest and not taking anything for granted, I'm sure doing an awful lot of overthinking.

*Life is too short not to be happy.*

My momma used to say that to me when I was younger. The irony that she died so young is certainly not lost on me.

But one thing I can say about my momma is that she lived by that mantra, and the short time she *was* on this Earth, she was happy.

Maybe I need to rip a page out of her playbook and stop finding excuses not to be happy. After all, I really have missed Jessie.

He's still looking at me as my mind wages battle with it-self. He's moved his hand off the door as if expected me to still walk through it.

The look on his face shows defeat as though he's worried he's already lost me.

This time, it's me who leans in to whisper, "I love you too, Jessie."

His head snaps up to look at me. Then, before I can even read the look on his face, he lifts me, wrapping my legs around him and trapping me between him and the door.

He devours me with his kiss. I moan into his mouth as his hands run through my hair. When he moves down to kiss my neck, the little bit of scruff on his cheeks rubs against my skin, making it tingle with need.

His head slowly moves up, so he's gazing into my eyes. "Do you know how long I've waited to hear you say that?"

Without waiting for me to respond, he carries me to his bedroom. Tossing me gently onto the bed, he quickly takes off his clothes. When it comes time for me to get undressed, though, he takes his time. His fingers glide across my skin as he pulls each garment from my body. As each item comes off, he trails kisses along the newly bare skin.

He teases me with his tongue, bringing it painfully close to my most sensitive areas but never actually touching them.

My fingers fist in his hair as I attempt to stay still. I'm not doing a very good job of it, though, as my body squirms beneath him.

"You better sit still, baby girl, or I'll have to tie you down," he warns.

"Then, give me what I want," I plead.

"Tell me what you want. *Exactly* what you want."

"Fuck me," I whimper. "Now!"

Without hesitation, he does what I ask, sliding into me in one swift motion. It's a tight fit, but he buries himself com-pletely. It's like after all these years, my pussy remembers him and contours around him perfectly.

Jessie moves inside me while kissing my neck and chest before moving down to lick and suck on my nipples. He circles the small nub with his tongue, and my pussy grows wetter.

My nails dig into his shoulders, and my legs wrap around him, pulling him closer. Our breaths turn ragged as our bodies slick with sweat.

His lips begin to kiss mine once more, and it feels so much more than every other kiss we've ever had.

More special.

More filled with love.

More passionately.

Just *more.*

We've gone far past the realm of just fucking, although I love doing that too. Instead, this is pouring all of our feelings into making love.

As we continue in our state of bliss, Jessie continues to tell me how much he loves me. It feels so insanely perfect that I can't believe I ever doubted it for a single moment. Everything seems so right.

So, we lie there. Locked in the moment. And I never want to leave.

# Chapter Twenty-two

## JESSIE

"Do you know how beautiful you are?" I ask Tracy as I gaze at her naked body next to me.

She chuckles. "You still have on your sex goggles."

"Sex goggles?"

"Yeah. Sex goggles. You ever heard of beer goggles?"

I nod. "Duh."

"Well, just like you drink a lot of beer and a *five* might suddenly turn into a *ten?* Your penis gives you sex goggles. It makes you think someone's more attractive than they really are so that it can get some action. Your penis clouds your vision."

When I look at her to see if she's serious, she busts out laughing.

"I hate to break it to you, baby girl," I begin. "But my dick just saw some action, and I still think you're the most gorgeous woman I've ever seen."

"Psssh. I know your penis, and it's *always* looking for some action."

My laugh booms in the room around us. "Although that may be true, my woman seems to enjoy it just as much as I do. In fact, she isn't afraid to tell me exactly *when* and *how* she likes to be fucked."

Leaning forward, I nip at the sensitive skin just below her

jawline.

The noise she makes lets me know I'm turning her on again, but she still pushes me away."

"Wild child, if you want to go again, I'm going to need food. I'm starving."

"You're always starving," I quip and continue to kiss.

"Food," she moans.

"Okay, okay," I concede. "Come on."

I stand up to throw my boxers back on, but she grabs my arm. "Keep the underwear off."

"You want me to cook naked?"

She gives me an excited grin and nods her head.

"Okay, but you're coming with me." Then, in one swift motion, I lift her, tossing her over my shoulder, carrying her to the couch, and plopping her down.

I walk to the fridge and glance inside. Unfortunately, I don't have a hell of a lot.

Milk. Eggs. Bacon. And a shit-ton of condiments.

When I name everything off to her, she asks, "Damn, what do you eat? You can't make too many meals out of that."

I shake my head. "I don't want to tell you. You'll laugh."

"Jessie, I'm already laughing. So, you might as well tell me," she responds.

"Well, I typically try to avoid the Stop 'N Go, so I eat at Jonas's a lot, and once a week, Momma brings me over some meals. I don't ask her to, but somehow, she still ends up over here every week."

Tracy smiles. "No judgment here. I think it's sweet that she does that for you."

"Yeah, she's sweet, but if you don't mind, I'd really like to *not* talk about my mother while my dick is over here flopping in the wind. It's just weird."

"Fair enough." She giggles. "How about some bacon?"

"Bacon?" I look down at my groin. "You want me to cook bacon naked? Remember how we just talked about my dick swinging around. Grease is a bad idea!"

Now, she's laughing so hard she snorts. It's adorable.

"I'm just kidding,' she says, wiping tears from her cheeks. "But it was too much fun not to suggest."

"Oh, haha," I reply. "My penis doesn't think you're very funny."

"I'll make it up to it." She winks.

When her eyes drift down to my lower half and she licks her lips, instantly, blood starts to flow, and I begin to get hard.

Fuck. Just one look from this woman has me standing at attention.

"Food," she reminds me.

"Right. I think I have some popcorn." Pulling out the box from the cabinet, I see there's one bag left.

"Popcorn sounds good," she says.

I spend the next few minutes cooking it and pouring it into a bowl. When I'm done, I join her on the couch, handing her the bowl. She digs in, and I cover us both up with a blanket.

We're quiet for a few minutes before I say, "So, I told you my big ol' sob story about what happened with me while we were apart. What happened with you? I mean, besides the business. I've got that part down."

She shrugs. "Honestly, there's not a whole lot to tell. I worked a lot. Had to work like crazy to save up enough money for a down payment for the store."

"Well, I imagine that it wasn't all work and no play. You told me you weren't a monk," I press.

"Ah, I see. So, you're asking me about my dating life." it comes out as a statement rather than a question.

"Sorry," I say. "You don't have to tell me. I'm just nosy."

"It's alright." She takes another bite of popcorn. "That wasn't all that exciting either. Did I date? Yes. Did I hook up with some of those guys? Sure. And no, I'm not going to give you my *number.* There was only one guy I was somewhat serious with."

"Who was he?" I ask, still being nosy.

"His name is Trent. He lives a couple of towns over. We met because his sister used to work at the shop. We were good for a while, even practically living together. But it didn't last."

"What happened?"

She sighs. "The same thing that always happens. Guys always seem to have an issue with some part of my life. They don't like that I'd rather be a business owner rather than a stay-at-home mom." She pauses to add, "I respect the hell out of women who make that choice, but I love my job, and I don't want to give it up.

"Anyways, other guys didn't like that I'm not exactly *ladylike*. I think that they were just jealous that I could shoot a gun and shotgun a beer better than they could. One didn't like the fact that I used the word *fuck*."

"So, which guy was Trent?"

"Trent lost his job, and his ego couldn't take that I was bringing in more money than he was. So, he'd bitch about everything. My hair. My clothes. My language. I kicked his ass to the curb pretty quick after that. I felt that I was leaving him when he was clearly down on his luck, but I wasn't going to stay and be his emotional punching bag either."

"You don't sound too heartbroken about it," I say.

She shrugs. "I mean, it sucks when every guy tries to change something fundamental about you, but at the end of the day, I'm not changing who I am. Every guy says he wants a strong, independent woman...until he actually gets one."

Tracy Kennedy is the strongest woman I know, and it makes my blood boil knowing so many tried to change her.

"Well, T," I say. "I've got some good news for you."

"Oh yeah?"

'Yep. See, you're never going to have to deal with one of those pricks ever again. Because I'm pretty set on keeping you all to myself from now on."

She smiles. "I'm going to hold you to that, wild child."

"Good." I kiss her hand. "Because I'm not going to let you down."

She sets the almost empty bowl on the coffee table and stands up. I gawk at her naked body as she stretches. My eyes move from her cute breasts with perky nipples to her thick hips and ass, and eventually on her neatly trimmed public hair that matches the auburn color on her head. I can see her pretty pussy lips under the thin hair.

A loud yawn comes out of her mouth, and I mentally tell my libido to calm down. I'm sure Tracy wants to get some sleep.

"You ready for bed, baby girl?" I ask.

She nods and starts heading that way. Stopping midway, she turns around. "Hey Jess, I've got good news too. I don't have to be at the store until tomorrow afternoon, so we can go to bed, but I'm not ready to go to sleep just yet." She gives me a wicked smile before heading back toward the bedroom.

Her ass jiggles as she walks, and instantly, my cock springs to life.

*Oh yeah. Tracy Kennedy is fucking perfect.*

# Chapter Twenty-three

## TRACY

Despite being able to sleep in this morning, I'm still tired all day at work. Jessie and I spent all night wrapped up in the sheets, getting to know each other's bodies all over again. I lost track of how many times we did it, but I know it was enough to still practically feel him between my legs.

Whenever I think about it, my pussy pulses with need, but I tell it to knock it off since it will not see any action tonight. Jessie has to work at the bar and won't get off until late. After sleeping next to him all week, it'll be weird to sleep alone again.

At least I'll be able to catch up on my sleep. I'm so tired I can barely keep my eyes open. And not surprisingly, my patience is practically non-existent. Because of that, I let the two girls I had working tonight go home early. They're sweet as can be, but I wasn't in the mood for the high-school gossip they were exchanging. I'd rather handle things myself and bask in the silence. I even shut off the music for the evening.

It's not been too busy, so I've been filling displays with new products. I doubt I'll get it all done, but I'm trying to make a dent before we close because the moment I switch that sign off, I'm heading home.

Pulling my phone out of my pocket, I look for a response from my dad. I texted him earlier to see if he was doing alright or if I needed to stop by and help him with anything. But it's been hours, and I've heard nothing.

I punch in the numbers for his cell phone, but instead of it ringing, it goes straight to voicemail. My heart starts to pound as every awful scenario plays in my head. Finally, I hang up and dial his home number.

I bite at my fingernails as the phone rings and rings. It's about six rings in when I finally hear a ragged, "Hello?"

"Dad?"

"Trace? What's wrong?" He sounds like he just woke up.

"I don't know. You tell me. I tried texting and calling your cell, and you didn't answer."

"Oh, that stupid thing? Somehow, I set the alarm on it, and every day, it'd go off at the same time. Finally, I got tired of hearing it, and today, I couldn't get the damn thing to shut off. So, I threw it against the wall and broke it."

I groan. "Dad, *I'm* the one who set that alarm. It's supposed to be your reminder to take your blood pressure medicine."

"Well, why didn't you tell me that?"

Sighing, I reply, "I *did*. And I texted you about it, and I left a note on the kitchen counter."

He scoffs so loudly I hold the phone away from my ear. "I don't need a reminder to take my medicine. I remember just fine. And you know what really raises my blood pressure? A damn alarm going off!"

My hand rubs my face listening to his stubbornness. "Dad, I just worry about you," I begin.

He cuts me off. "Darlin', isn't it my job to worry about *you?*"

I hold my tongue to avoid telling him that I was still practically taking care of him while I was still living at home. That desire to help hasn't gone away. In fact, it got even stronger when he started having health problems.

He pulls me from my thoughts. "I'm fine. I promise. Now, I'll talk to you later."

Before I can protest any further, he hangs up the phone. His stubbornness makes me miss my momma. She always had a way of getting through to him.

I love my father. He's a good, hardworking man. He took care of me the best way that he knew how after Momma died. He was never overly affectionate, but then again, neither was I. I never begged for his attention because I was always out setting the world ablaze while he was always working.

I'm sure that I had my own way of getting under his skin when I'd do something stupid and get into trouble. But he never stayed mad for long.

He had no idea how to raise a little girl all alone, but he did his best. When he did have free time, he'd take me hunting or fishing—activities that didn't require a whole lot of talking but still allowed us to spend time together.

Sighing, I force myself off the road down memory lane and glance at the clock. Only fifteen minutes to go until I could go home and crash.

*Thank goodness.*

\*\*\*\*\*\*\*\*\*\*\*\*\*\*\*\*\*\*\*\*\*\*\*\*\*\*\*\*\*\*\*\*\*\*\*\*\*\*\*\*\*\*\*\*\*\*\*\*\*\*\*\*\*\*\*\*\*\*\*\*\*\*\*\*

My eyes shoot open when I hear something outside. Sitting straight up, I glance around, trying to get my bearings. My chest heaves, but I try to quiet it so I can hear better.

*Maybe I just dreamed it.*

But the moment my head hits the pillow again, I hear the noise once more—only this time, it sounds like someone is trying to open my front door.

Glancing at the clock, I see it's after midnight. Jessie told me he wouldn't be off until after two.

*Who the fuck?*

Not waiting for the bastard to make his way inside, I jump out of bed and grab the shotgun I keep in my closet. I don't turn on any lights, and I pad across my wooden floors as to not let the bastard know I'm onto him.

My eyes catch a glimpse of the shadow outside the living room window. Wearing nothing more than a tank top and my underwear, I set one hand on the doorknob, ready to swing it open and charge into the night.

Taking a deep breath, I don't allow any extra time to think.

Instead, I yank open the door and cock the shotgun.

"Freeze!" I yell.

I'm surprised as hell when it's Jessie on the other end of the barrel.

"Whoa, T!" He cries, throwing his hands in the air.

"Jessie, what the fuck?! I thought you were working until two!"

"It was slow, so I got off early and thought I'd surprise you!"

"By trying to break in?" I shriek.

"I figured you'd have a spare key or something. Or that the door would be unlocked. I swear you're the only person who keeps their door locked in this Podunk town."

"Well, that's not going to stop *now*."

"Can we maybe have this conversation when you're not pointing a gun at me?!"

I realize I'm still holding the shotgun firmly locked on him. "Oh, right. Sorry."

Lowering the gun, I cock it once more so that the unused shell pops out, and I catch it with my free hand.

Jessie eyes me up and down. "I don't know whether to be terrified or turned on."

Rolling my eyes, I laugh. "Come on, let's go inside. I'm sure Miss Marlow has been watching this whole thing, and I'm surprised she hasn't called the cops."

I lead him into the house and put the shotgun back in its place. Jessie follows me to the bedroom.

"Did you walk outside in just your panties?" He asks, peeking at my ass as I bend over.

"I thought someone was breaking in. I wasn't about to waste time putting on pants," I retort. I crawl in bed before adding, "So, you came over here to see me?"

He shrugs. "I kind of missed you."

"Just kind of?" I smile, pulling him down for a kiss.

Once I pull back, he says, "I want you to know that I didn't come here for that. I figured you'd be tired, and I was just going to cuddle you."

"Well, wild child, you've got my heart pumping, and I don't think I'm going to get much sleep for a while."

I say it like I'm complaining, but honestly, I'm happy he's here. I missed him too.

"Wide awake, huh? Let's see what we can do about that." He pulls off his clothes until he's down to his boxers. As the bed sinks beneath his knees, he says, "I'm *very* hungry."

The words may sound innocent, but the way he's looking my body up and down, I can tell that food isn't what he's referring to.

His eyes stay locked on mine as he crawls between my legs and slips off my underwear. Grabbing a pillow, he positions it under my ass so that I'm perfectly on display for him. As he gets himself comfortable, his eyes move down my body until they're firmly fixed on my wet center.

When we were teenagers, Jessie loved to eat my pussy, doing it as foreplay almost every time we had sex. I always loved it—even when I didn't come.

My clit is throbbing with need, and I wonder if he can see it pulsing as he gazes upon me.

He trails kisses along my thighs, moving closer each time to exactly where I need it but never actually getting there. My eyes squeeze shut as I struggle to sit still.

I feel him spread me even wider, his fingers opening me for him. I let out a loud moan as I finally feel his tongue make contact with my clit. He pulls back the hood to expose my most sensitive area.

"Holy shit!" I cry as he sucks it into his mouth. He continues the sucking motion while licking circles around it.

My legs are already starting to shake, and I know this isn't going to take long. The man has always been enthusiastic in the oral sex department, but the years have improved his technique.

My core starts to tighten as I can feel the impending storm beginning to brew. Jessie makes a humming noise against my clit, causing a slight vibration, which only adds to everything.

My pussy is so wet I can practically feel it dripping. He takes two of his fingers and slips them inside my channel. They glide in with ease, and he angles them upward to massage my g-spot.

It's less than a minute before all the sensations became too much. Heat spreads like wildfire from my core through my entire body. My fingers tangle in Jessie's hair as I hold him still, riding out my release on his face. Instinctively, my thighs try to squeeze together, and I worry I might squish his head in between them.

He continues devouring me like I'm his last meal until he's pulled every ounce of pleasure from me, and I'm too sensitive for more. He gives me one final long lick with his tongue before moving to lie beside me.

"Wow," I whisper, my chest heaving.

He pulls me close to him and lays my head on his chest. "Come here, beautiful," he whispers.

His fingers run through my hair and gently massage my scalp. I'm already feeling myself starting to fall asleep, but I don't want to leave Jessie hanging.

Lazily, I run my hands down his stomach to the waistband of his boxers. Judging from the tent he's sporting, I can tell he's hard, but his hand stops mine.

"Baby girl, I'm fine. You're tired." He kisses the top of my head. "Let's just get some sleep."

I'm about to tell him that I'm wide awake, but my heavy eyelids are winning the battle.

So, instead, I just murmur, "Okay, sweets. I owe you one."

# Chapter Twenty-four

## JESSIE

"Hey, Jessie!" Andi greets, opening the front door. "Come on in."

She moves out of the way, and I step inside.

"How are you, Andi?" I ask.

"Pretty good, I guess. Can't complain. How are things with you?"

"Same."

She walks around, picking up random toys that are scattered everywhere. "So, what brings you here on a Saturday?"

"Oh, just wondering if my grumpy big brother is around."

She giggles. "He's not grumpy."

"Maybe not to you. He knows better than that, I'm sure."

She gives me a warm smile. "True. He's out back playing with the boys."

"Thanks." I nod and head toward the back of the house.

When I walk through the screen door, I see my oldest brother playing football with his two foster sons. Jonas runs slowly so that both boys can tackle him and steal the ball.

I've always known Jonas would be a good dad and seeing him with those two confirms it even more. He and Andi care for the boys as though they were their own kids. Aw, hell, what am I saying? Those boys *are* their own kids now.

Jonas notices me and tells the boys to go practice without

him for a few minutes. They do as they're told, and he walks up on the deck to join me.

'Hey, Jess," he greets. "What are you doing here?"

That's a loaded question because I'm here to do something I never thought I would.

"Can't I just come over to see my brother?" I ask.

He laughs. "I guess you could, but that would mean Hell has frozen over, and I don't think that's happened. So, why don't you cut the shit and tell me why you're really here?"

"That's fair," I mutter. "I'm here...to ask you if that offer for a job is still valid."

His eyes go wide. "Okay, I'm going to call Momma because Hell really *is* freezing over."

I roll my eyes. "Haha. Very funny."

He chuckles at his joke for a moment before asking, "Why the sudden change of heart?"

I shrug and try to sound cool, "Well, the bar doesn't always give me a steady income which makes it hard to save up to plan for anything. It'd be nice to have a—"

He cuts me off. "That sounds like the *right* reason. Why don't you tell me the *real* reason?"

Tracy's face pops into my mind. "I'm sure you already know the real reason."

"Tracy?"

I nod.

"Is she giving you shit for working at the bar?" He asks.

I'm a bit taken aback by his question. "No. She doesn't even know I'm here asking you for a job. It's more than that."

He doesn't speak but instead waits for me to continue.

"Joe, I let Tracy go a long time ago, and I don't intend on making that mistake again. I want to give her everything she wants and needs. It's hard to do that when we're on entirely different schedules. I want to give her a good life, but it's hard to do that when I don't know how much money I'll bring in each day. I need something more stable." I groan. "I sound ridiculous, don't I?"

"No, not ridiculous at all. Trust me; I know what it's like to be willing to move Heaven and Earth for the woman you love." He looks inside at his wife, who is dancing around in the kitchen while she does the dishes. "Of course, you have a job here. You're family."

"Thanks, Joe."

"You're welcome. How about you start on Wednesday next week? I have to go out of town Monday and Tuesday, but I can show you the ropes when I get back."

"Sounds great, man."

"Not to pry, but have you told Tracy about everything that happened in Nashville?"

Nodding, I say, "Yep. I told her everything, and surprisingly, she didn't run screaming in the other direction."

"Sounds like a keeper. Hold onto her. You don't know how special that is."

My thoughts run wild with Tracy. "Oh, trust me. I really do."

# Chapter Twenty-five

## TRACY

"So, I guess you should be thanking me, huh?" Jamie asks me while hanging up some clothes.

It's been a while since she and I have worked together. Since she acts as manager when I'm not here, I try to stagger our shifts. And two days a week, we have one other girl who is in charge to help pick up the slack.

"What the hell should I be thankful for?" I ask, eyes wide.

"See, if I hadn't set you up on that awful blind date, you wouldn't have gone to The Saddle and saw Jessie. And you guys never would have gotten back together."

In a way, she's right. I'm thankful for the way things worked out. It all seemed rather kismet. But in another way, I think Jessie and I still somehow would have found our way back to each other.

Not wanting to admit that she might have a point, I instead tell her to shut it.

I decide to change the subject. "How are things with biker boy?"

She practically swoons. "Wonderful. Well, the sex anyway. That's about all we do. To be honest, it's the only thing we have in common."

"Sounds romantic." My words drip with sarcasm.

"Oh, you're one to talk. You're the least romantic person

that I know," she argues.

I scoff. "I may not be all into chocolates and flowers, but at least my man and I do other things besides just screw?'

"So, you *are* screwing?"

*Shit! I walked right into that one.*

"Something like that," I respond, trying to keep it vague.

"Well, don't look now, but I think your loverboy just walked through the door," she teases.

I'm convinced she's just blowing me shit, so I about jump out of my skin when I hear a deep voice behind me.

"Hey there, gorgeous."

When I turn around, he laughs. "Jamie just told you I was here."

"I didn't believe her," I say, and before he can question further, I add, "Don't ask."

He just shoots me that million-dollar smile. "Can I steal you away for a few minutes to talk?"

My heart pounds with a mix of excitement and worry. "Sure, let's go in the back to my office."

He gestures for me to lead the way. I ask Jamie to watch over things for a few minutes, and we head to the back.

Once in there, I shut the door, and we sit down in the two chairs.

Jessie looks around and lets out a soft chuckle. When I ask what's so funny, he responds with, "Your office is just like you. Chaotic. Yet somehow all perfectly put together."

I can't help but smile. "Are you trying to butter me up before we have this little talk of yours?"

"Nope. Just trying to charm the pants off you." He winks, and I immediately am picturing both of us without pants. "But I actually came here with some good news. Well, at least I think it's good."

I interrupt his rambling. "Okay, Jess. Spill it."

"I quit my job at the bar," he blurts.

I'm not entirely sure how to react because that seems like a somewhat impulsive decision.

He says, "Wait, can I start over? I sort of had a whole speech planned."

"Sure."

"Okay," he begins, taking a deep breath. "I realized last night after coming to your house and almost getting shot that you and I are on two *very* different schedules, and that would make spending time together more difficult. But here's the thing, I don't want that to be more difficult. I'd like to go sleep with you by my side every night—if you'll let me, of course."

"I'd like that too," I reply honestly. "But you just quit your job?"

"Yes. Well, kind of. I asked Jonas for a job on the ranch."

My eyes go wide because I'm not sure how great it is for Jonas and Jessie to work together. That's like mixing oil and water.

Jessie must notice the shock on my face because he says, "Yeah, I know. But it would be nice to have a job with a steady income and a better schedule."

My hand reaches out to grab his. "You don't have to do this for me, you know?"

He brings my hand to his mouth and kisses it. "I know that. I'm doing this for *us.* I don't have to work at the ranch forever, but it'll get me by for now."

I smile. "You're sweet. Do you know that?"

He scoots a little closer. "Oh yeah? How sweet?"

I shrug. "Let's just say that it makes me like you a little."

Grabbing my face in his hands, he says, "Well, I have news for you, baby girl. I'm head over heels in love with you, so get used to it."

Now, I'm not a girl who swoons. Ever. It takes a whole hell of a lot to get through all of my tough layers to get down to the sweet, soft center.

But damnit if Jessie Mitchell hasn't drilled through all those layers right down to my core.

I lean forward and kiss him. It's not overly sexual or passionate. But it is filled with love.

Once I pull back and look at him, I ask, "So, when do you start the new job?"

"Wednesday. I was scheduled to work tonight and tomorrow, but when I talked to Al, he said Sadie had something happen with her car and was begging for more hours. So, I let her take my remaining shifts." He smiles. "Plus, it'll give me a couple of extra days with my woman. But you probably have to work, huh?"

"I work today, but then, I'm off the next couple. What do you want to do?"

He grins and wiggles his eyebrows at me. "You know what I want to do."

Without waiting, he pulls me out of my chair and onto his lap.

Giggling, I respond, "Well, yeah, we are going to do *that.* But what else?"

His arms hold me tight. "I thought that maybe we could get out of town for a couple of days."

I feel a bit conflicted because I don't leave Grady often— really ever. Grady is my home base, and I love it here. But I can't imagine what it's like for Jessie. People haven't been exactly welcoming since he's been back, so it's probably not all that 'homey' for him.

Getting away with him for a few days might be good for him.

"Okay, where do you want to go?" I ask.

"You tell me. I'll take you wherever you want."

I think for a moment before answering, "Let's just drive until we find somewhere to stop. We will just wing it."

His perfect teeth show as he laughs. "You're a little bit crazy. Do you know that?"

I nod and whisper in his ear, "You love it."

"Fuck yes, I do."

He kisses me again—this time, hard and fast. My fingers snake through his hair, and I turn my body so that I'm straddling him.

Our kiss intensifies, and I feel him getting hard beneath me. Slowly, I grind my pelvis against him. His fingertips dig into my ass as I moan into his mouth.

With a bit of force, he pulls my hair, tilting my head back and breaking our kiss.

Breathing heavily, he says, "Baby girl, as much as I want to fuck you right now—and believe me, I *will* bend you over this desk one day—I'll do it when there's not a store full of people out there. I don't want anyone else to hear the noises you make. Those are all for me."

The thought of him bending me over my desk turns me on, and the idea of people hearing turns me on even more. Is that weird?

I don't care.

"I'll let you get back to work," he says. "How about I come over tonight when you get home, and we can leave in the morning?"

I nod. "Sounds good, sweets."

I get up off his lap, and he adjusts himself to hide his hard-on.

As he's leaving, he adds, "I love you, T. So fucking much."

*Oh yeah. I'm definitely swooning.*

# Chapter Twenty-six

## JESSIE

I pull my truck up in the dirt driveway in front of my momma's house. Typically, we have a big family dinner on Sundays, but since Tracy and I are going on our little road trip, I'll have to miss this one. So, I'm here to beg for forgiveness.

I'm a little surprised she doesn't come out to greet me. Usually, she's on that porch the moment she hears someone pull onto the drive.

Getting out of the truck, I walk up the flower-lined walkway toward the front door. I take a moment to look up at the big house I grew up in. Momma inherited the house from her father. He moved a couple of towns over, and this place became our home.

It's a beautiful old farmhouse. Although it needs some work, Momma tries her best to keep it looking nice. And my brothers and I help whenever we can.

Swinging open the tattered screen door, I hear country music coming from the kitchen. No wonder Momma didn't hear me drive up.

The moment I'm inside, my nostrils fill with the smell of freshly baked banana bread. It smells amazing.

I walk through the open entryway and veer left into the kitchen where's she's doing the dishes and singing to herself.

When I flick the radio off, she whips around so fast that

she sloshes water everywhere. Her hand grips her chest, leaving a wet handprint.

"Jessie Cole, you about scared me half to death!" She cries.

"Sorry, Momma," I throw my hands up. "Didn't mean to startle you."

She wipes her hands on a dishtowel. "Oh, it's alright. I'm happy you're here all the same. Are you hungry?"

"Nah, I'm alright." I take a seat at the small table on the other side of the kitchen.

As if not even listening to me, she cuts a slice of banana bread, spreads some butter on it, and sets it in front of me.

The woman always makes sure I will never starve.

"Thanks, Momma."

"So, what are you doing here? Don't get me wrong, I'm glad to see you, but I think I heard from you more when you lived in Nashville." There's no mistaking the snark in her tone.

"I'm sorry. I should be better about calling and coming by. After all, you still keep me fed all the time." I decide it's better not to feed her a bunch of bullshit. She'd probably never believe it anyway.

She's suspicious of my groveling too, though. "Okay, what do you want?"

"You sound like Jonas. Why do I have to want something?"

"Because, Jessie, even on your best days, you're still a sarcastic son-of-a-gun."

I chuckle at her refusal ever to curse.

She asks again. "So, tell me what brings you here."

Picking at the banana bread and avoiding eye contact, I say, "I need to miss family dinner tomorrow night."

"Why?"

"I'm going out of town for a couple of days."

"Oh?" That's a loaded 'oh' because it's laced with worry that I'm on my way back to Nashville to get into trouble.

"Well, I'm sure you have heard through the grapevine that Tracy Kennedy and I have started seeing each other again."

She leans back in her chair. "Maybe. But I'd like to hear the real story from you."

I'm not quite sure even where to start. I'm pretty sure anything I say will earn me a lecture from her, so I just say, "Momma, I love her. I know it sounds soon, but I feel like we are just picking up right where we left off. She's so smart and funny and just so amazing. She's the one, Momma."

I brace for impact from her verbal tongue lashing.

She surprises me, though, when she says, "It's about damn time."

I choke on my bread. "Momma, you cursed!"

"I think the lord will understand in this case."

"You're not going to give me some sort of lecture about jumping the gun? Or how I should focus on my recovery instead of chasing tail?"

She stands up to pour herself another cup of coffee. The woman drinks black coffee from sunup to sundown.

"Jessie, Tracy Kennedy is a good girl. She's the kind of a girl a mother wishes for her son. There's not a single doubt in my mind that she'll help your sobriety, not wreck it."

"Can I ask you something?" I take another bite.

"No."

My head whips to look at her, and she laughs.

"I'm just kidding. Shoot."

"Do you think if Tracy and I would've stayed together back then, I would have still gone down the rough road that I did? Do you think I would've made all those stupid decisions?"

She waves her finger at me. "It's not going to do any good to dwell on questions like that. You can't change the past. You can only learn from it. And honestly, if you two stayed together back then, it probably wouldn't have lasted—or it would have, but it wouldn't be good like it is now."

"What do you mean?"

"I mean, y'all were just kids. You'd only been with each other, and you hadn't experienced the world. Now, you have, and you still found your way back to each other. So, I'd say that's pretty dang special."

I'm quiet for a few moments, trapped in my thoughts, before saying, "I don't want to ever hold her back. Tracy's like a wild mare. She shouldn't be tamed."

"Then, *don't* hold her back. Help her. Support her however you can. Just be there and be the man she fell in love with. Never stop trying to be better."

My momma seems always to know just what to say. The woman has been through hell and back, and yet she's always there for her kids no matter what.

In a low voice, I say, "I'm really sorry."

"For what?"

"For turning out just like Daddy. For letting you down. For messing up the plan."

She laughs. "Honey, I have four kids. I learned a long time ago that it's pointless to always have a plan. You'll just be disappointed."

"But I was all set. I was on track to get a scholarship with a full ride to wherever I wanted. Then, when I got into trouble, all of that went away."

"Jessie, you were a good swimmer—a *great* swimmer. But it's not like you ever really *loved* it. I think you just did it because you were good at it. Who cares that you didn't stick with it? You got some life experience—even though it taught you some harsh lessons.

"But you listen to me, Jessie Cole; you could never let me down. You're my baby boy—no matter what. You just lost your way for a little while, but I don't think you're like your daddy."

"Everyone else in this town seems to think I am," I insist.

"Everyone else in this town doesn't even know what went on between your daddy and me. They just have their *perception* of what happened. At the end of the day, your daddy had a sickness—a disease. His addiction turned him into a different person. And his addiction eventually killed him. The difference between you two? You got better. You work at staying that way every day. I loved your daddy. God rest his soul, but he's gone. You're here. You're alive. So, you just live your life the best way you know how."

"How do you always know the right thing to say?" I ask.

"Four kids!" She laughs. "I've had many crazy talks with your brothers too—and now your sister."

'I'm sure I gave you the biggest headaches."

"Maybe out of the boys, but your sister is going to give you a run for your money." She winks. "But I think you've always been the kid that's the sweetest to me."

I think about how I haven't always been sweet to her, but now I will always do my best to be a good son.

She interrupts my thoughts, "And I don't care if you miss dinner tomorrow. How about you bring Tracy over next week to join us?"

I smile. "I'd like that, and I'm sure she would too."

My attention turns toward the footsteps walking into the kitchen. My sister, Jenna, walks in with her hair piled in a messy bun on top of her head.

"Hey, Jen," I greet.

"Hi," she says with a big eye roll. "Mom, I'm going for a walk."

She's out the door before either one of us can say another word, so Momma yells, "Be back before dark!"

She turns back toward me. "If you don't make things right with her soon, I'm coming to live with you."

"I will. I promise."

I mean it too. When I leave shortly after our talk, I drive around looking for Jenna but have no luck. If she's anything like I was, she's off partying in the woods.

When we get back from our little trip, I promise myself Jenna and I will finally hash things out.

For now, it's off to see my woman.

# Chapter Twenty-seven

## JESSIE

"I'm sorry I fell asleep last night," Tracy apologizes for the third time.

We've been on the road for about an hour, driving down back roads, leading nowhere in particular.

I reach over to the cab of the truck and take her hand in mine. "Will you stop apologizing? You were tired. It's not a big deal."

"I just feel bad. I was looking forward to your naughty time."

"T, we are going to have plenty of time for that. I promise. The moment we stop for the night, I'm going to do filthy things to your naked body."

She looks at me with a twinkle in her eye. "I've got another idea."

Before I can ask what it is, she's scooting closer to me. Then, her hand begins rubbing my thigh up and down. With each pass, she gets closer to my dick.

And my dick takes notice, getting hard and testing the material of my jeans.

When she reaches over with her other hand to help undo the zipper, my eyes go wide. She pulls it out and strokes me up and down.

"Baby girl, what are you doing?" I ask, struggling to

breathe.

"Having fun." She smiles before leaning over. Then, getting comfortable, she runs her tongue along the purple head. God, this is the wild Tracy Kennedy I remember—always up for a good time even if it meant getting in a bit of trouble along the way.

"I'm trying to drive, beautiful."

"Keep driving. Besides, we are in the middle of nowhere."

She's right. I haven't seen another car in miles on this old country road, but I slow down all the same.

Doing my best to keep my eyes on the road, I feel Tracy take the length of me down her throat.

"Holy shit, T," I groan.

She takes me down as far as she can before pulling back swirling her tongue around the head. Finally, she gets on her knees, so her plump ass is up in the air, and it takes every ounce of me not to gawk at it. Later on, I'm going to put her in this exact position while I fuck her.

She continues to give me head, and every time I come close to filling up her mouth, she slows down. She brings me right to the edge, teasing me every time before changing her tempo.

"Fuck, T!" I growl.

My balls start to tighten, and as good as that mouth of hers is, I crave more. Turning the wheel, I pull the truck off to the side of the road.

Once it's come to a complete stop, I throw it in park and grab Tracy's head, pulling her up to look at me before devouring her with my kiss.

"Take off your pants," I command when both of us are breathless.

She wastes no time shimmying out of her shorts and panties.

"Come here." I scoot the seat back, so I'm not as close to the wheel, and pull her into my lap.

She sinks onto me, her wet pussy sucking me in and squeezing me. When she begins to move, she rides my dick like her life depends on it.

Tugging down her tank top, I take one of her cute pink nipples in my mouth. She cries out when I gently nip at it with my teeth.

I worry I'm hurting her until she says, "Harder. Bite it harder."

I do as she asks, and her screams echo in the truck all around us. My fingers grab her hips as I thrust harder into her.

Pretty soon, we are both coming at the same time. And good lord, it's incredible.

When her body stills on top of me, I run my fingers through her hair and kiss her once more.

Resting my forehead against hers, I say, "Damn, baby girl. You're going to kill me."

"I was okay with just taking care of you—not that I'm complaining. But I figured I owed you after you took care of me the other night," she says while scooting over and sliding her shorts back on.

"Hey, you listen to me." I tilt her chin, so her eyes stare into mine. "You don't owe me shit. That's not how this works. Every time you let me between those gorgeous legs of yours, I consider it a privilege, whether I'm getting anything in return or not."

She gives me a genuine smile.

"So, where to, beautiful?" I ask, pulling the truck back onto the road.

She giggles. "Just drive."

\*\*\*\*\*\*\*\*\*\*\*\*\*\*\*\*\*\*\*\*\*\*\*\*\*\*\*\*\*\*\*\*\*\*\*\*\*\*\*\*\*\*\*\*\*\*\*\*

"Why are you dancing around?" I look over at Tracy, who can't seem to sit still.

"I have to pee."

"Why didn't you say something?" We stopped after our sex, and she ran into a gas station to pee and clean herself up, but that was a couple of hours ago. "We are coming up on Patterson. We'll find somewhere there to stop."

She cranks up the radio, giving her even more of a reason to dance around.

Once buildings and shops start to come into view, I start looking for a place to stop.

Tracy about scares the shit out of me when she exclaims, "Oh, look! A Cost Mart! Can we stop?"

"You want to stop at Cost Mart?" I ask. Cost Mart is one of those big warehouse-type stores that sells everything in bulk and that you need a membership to shop at.

She nods excitedly. "I've never been to one."

"And the thought of going to one excites you?"

"Jessie, you've seen how much I eat. Does a store that sells all sorts of junk food in bulk excite me? What do you think?"

I chuckle. "Whatever you want, baby girl."

I pull into the oversized parking lot and park the truck. As we hit the front doors, her eyes go wide.

"This place is huge," she murmurs under her breath.

Reminding her of her bladder, I point to the restroom while I head to get us a guest pass to shop for the day.

Once she's back, I grab us a cart, and we start walking around. Twenty minutes in, I realize we might need a second one because Tracy is grabbing everything in sight.

"They need to build a Cost Mart in Grady," she keeps saying.

"Pretty sure that would put the Stop 'N Go out of business."

"Exactly." She gives me a disgusted look. "Some days, I really hate that place."

"You and me both. That's why I try to avoid it at all costs. I can't believe you've never been to Cost Mart before. They were everywhere in Nashville."

She gives a weak smile. "I don't get out of Grady much, and when I do, it's always for work." She makes sure to add, "Not that I don't love Grady, I do."

I stop her before she gets too far in the weeds. "T, it's okay to love your hometown and still want to see other parts of the world occasionally."

There's no doubt Tracy Kennedy is small-town through

and through, and nothing will change that. But I'd love the opportunity to explore other places with her.

Grabbing her hand, I say, "How about this? Before we leave, we get a membership—a real membership. And you and I drive out here once a month to get all of your favorites. It'll get us away from Grady for an afternoon while stocking up. That means fewer trips to the Stop 'N Go. It's a win-win."

She grins. "Why are you so sweet?"

Leaning down, I kiss her. "Because you give me so much sugar."

She laughs and rolls her eyes. "Oh, geez! What a line!" Before she walks away, she playfully punches me in the shoulder.

Flattery might work with most women, but anything less than sincerity toward Tracy will get your ass kicked.

She's always been that way. When we were kids, I watched a boy give his 'girlfriend' a dandelion he picked from the grass. So, I decided to follow suit and do the same thing for Tracy. She took one look at it, scolded me for picking her a wildflower, and told me I needed to be more creative and not copy off someone else.

The memory makes me smile. She's been calling me on my bullshit for years. And I hope she keeps doing it for many more to come.

# Chapter Twenty-eight

## TRACY

After we leave Cost Mart with the truck full of all our goodies, I offer to drive for a while. Jessie hands over the keys without question, and we hit the road once more.

Our drive consists of mainly country roads with the occasional pass-through of a small town. The further East we go, the closer we get to the heart of the Smokey Mountains, and those small towns turn into bigger cities focused on tourism.

My parents brought me up to the mountains when I was younger. We'd go to Gatlinburg every year and do as much as possible in the few days we were there.

It was my momma's favorite place in the world. I think that's why Daddy and I never went back after she died. It just didn't seem right.

Honestly, that's probably why I haven't been anywhere. When I was little, she and I would talk about all the places we wanted to visit when I got older. We'd make big plans while we sat outside watching the sunset. She'd make us hot chocolate, and we'd snuggle up on the porch swing and dream about the places we wanted to go. Our list was a mile long.

And then, she died. And I never went anywhere. Traveling was something that reminded me of her. Considering I've done my best to avoid any type of feelings, doing something that reminded me of her didn't seem like a good idea.

I got so comfortable in Grady that I never wanted to leave, which is probably why I opposed the idea so adamantly when Jessie suggested leaving when we were younger.

"What's going on in that big ol' brain of yours?" Jessie asks. "You've been quiet for a while."

I consider lying, but I know he'll see right through me.

Sighing, I answer, "My mom."

He takes my hand in his. "What about your mom?"

"We used to talk about traveling a lot," I begin before explaining to him all the thoughts swimming around in my head.

When I'm done, he asks, "Do you think you want to start traveling now? I mean, it's not too late."

"I don't know," I answer honestly. "I'd love to see things, but I feel like I'm letting her down or something. I feel like she'd be sad that I did it without her."

"T—"

I cut him off. "I know that sounds crazy. Absolutely insane. She's dead. She can't feel *anything*."

"That's not what I was going to say." He looks at me. "I was going to say that I'm sure your mom would be happy that you're doing all the things she didn't get to. And maybe in some strange way, she'd be right there with you."

I've never been overly spiritual, so I've never thought much about that. When my mom died, I lost all faith in God and everything associated with him—the afterlife included.

And that sounds like a bit too much to try to unpack right now. This is supposed to be a fun, relaxing trip.

"So, where should we go?" I ask, changing the subject. "Are you ready to stop for the night?"

"We can do whatever you want, baby girl. You're driving." He smiles.

"Let's start looking for a hotel. A nice one...with room service. I'm starving."

He chuckles. "You're always starving." Pulling out his phone, he does an internet search for hotels near us. He finds one about twenty minutes away, so I head in that direction.

But halfway there, something catches my eye. Something that looks like a hell of a lot of fun.

Quickly, I turn the steering wheel and change direction. The hotel can wait.

*************************************************

"Are you okay?" I ask Jessie as the giant Ferris wheel carries us up to the top.

"I'm fine. Why?"

"Because you're squeezing my hand so hard that it's turning white."

His eyes flick down, and he loosens his grip. "Sorry," he mutters.

"What's wrong?"

His knee bobs up and down nervously. "I don't really like heights."

My eyes go wide. "Since when?"

"Since always."

My mind races with memories of our younger days. We were always doing adrenaline-filled things, and he never acted like he was scared of heights.

"Jessie, you and I have jumped off cliffs into lakes. We've biked down Devil's Hill. Why didn't you ever say anything?"

"Same reason I didn't say anything before we got on this spinning wheel of death. Because I was chasing after a beautiful woman. I'd follow you anywhere, T."

Lord, he makes me feel all warm and fuzzy inside—a feeling I'm not at all used to.

"That might be the sweetest thing I've ever heard," I say.

His eyes keep glancing out the metal cage we're in and down to the ground. Every time he does, his face shows every ounce of his anxiety.

"Hey," I get his attention. "Look at me."

He doesn't do it right away, so I grab his face and turn it toward me.

"Look at me—not the ground," I command. "Let me take your mind off of *the spinning wheel of death*."

Pulling him closer, I press my lips against his. At first, I can still feel his apprehension, but it doesn't take long for him to deepen the kiss. His fingers run through my hair, holding me in place while his tongue starts to explore my mouth.

My hands fist in his shirt as I wish so badly we were alone right now and not in a Ferris wheel in broad daylight. Every flick of his tongue fills my head with thoughts of that tongue doing other naughty things.

We get so lost in the moment that it seems like mere seconds pass when we hear someone clearing his throat.

Looking up, we see that we're back on the ground, and the ride attendant is impatiently waiting for us to step out.

"Sorry," I mouth as we exit the ride.

As we're walking back to the truck, Jessie wraps his arm around my shoulders. Then, grinning, he says, "If that's what we get to do on Ferris wheels, maybe they aren't so bad after all."

# Chapter Twenty-nine

## JESSIE

Once we are in our plush hotel room, Tracy and I decide to hop in the shower. I'm pretty sure I smell like nervous sweat from the whole Ferris wheel adventure.

The hot water feels amazing as we take time washing each other. I even take the time to shampoo her hair, massaging her scalp as she moans in pleasure.

I'm trying to keep my dick from getting hard because as sexy as Tracy is, shower sex is never all it's cracked up to be—especially with someone as tall as me and someone as short as her.

Instead, I kiss her, rub her, and lull her into a sense of complete relaxation.

When we're done, we dry off before putting on our big, fluffy robes, compliments of the hotel.

"Look at this giant bed!" Tracy squeals, crawling onto it and starting to jump up and down.

She giggles and looks like she's having the time of her life. I love the fact that she can enjoy the little things.

"Just don't hit your head on the ceiling, little monkey," I warn, grabbing the room service menu off the end table. "What do you want to eat?"

She stops jumping and plops down next to me so she can peruse the menu as well.

It takes less than thirty seconds for her to say, "Steak. The biggest one they have. And a baked potato."

"Do you want a salad?" I joke.

"I will kick your ass," she says with a laugh.

I pick up the phone and quickly place our order: two giant steaks and two baked potatoes.

Before I hang up, Tracy whispers, "See if they have mac and cheese."

After adding mac and cheese to the order, I hang up and pull her close to snuggle.

"Hey, T," I say, getting her to look up at me.

"Yeah?"

"Thanks for coming on this trip with me. I didn't realize that it might be hard on you until you started talking about your mom. I didn't know that it might be a hot button issue."

"You're welcome. It's actually been nice to get away with you. When we were kids, it was a hell of a lot harder to get out of town."

I kiss the top of her forehead. "Very true."

I feel her smile against me. "But we had some good times, though, didn't we?"

"We sure did. But to tell you the truth, T, I'm much more excited about all the memories we'll make in our future." I hand her the remote and let her pick something to watch.

After flipping through the channels for a few minutes before settling on some nature show, I start to drift off to sleep when there's a knock on the door.

Making sure my robe is securely fastened, I answer it and bring our dinners inside.

When I take the metal domes off the plates, two of the most enormous steaks I've ever seen come into view.

Tracy's eyes go wide as she sits down at the small table. "Get ready, wild child. You're about to see a magic trick."

I laugh, but over the next half hour, I see that she's not joking. And it *is* a damn magic trick. She eats every ounce of food in front of her. I have no idea where she's putting all of it. Hell, she eats more than I do.

I don't care what anyone says—a woman who isn't afraid to eat is sexy as fuck.

Once we are done eating, we cuddle up once again, but our eyes are both heavy this time. It doesn't take long before we both drift off.

I have no idea how long I've been asleep when I feel the front of my robe being pulled open. Small, warm hands tickle my balls and then move up to start stroking my dick.

My eyes slowly open to see Tracy working me up and down. The way she's looking at my dick like it's a damn work of art makes it grow even harder.

Letting go of it momentarily, she shrugs out of her robe and tosses it aside. Once she's naked, she leans forward on her knees and takes me in her mouth.

"Oh shit, baby girl," I moan as I hit the back of her throat. My eyes are glued to her ass sticking up in the air while her head bobs up and down.

Grabbing her hips, I turn her body. "Bring that ass here, baby girl. Let me see it."

She does as I command, and I have the perfect view of her round ass and pretty pussy. While she continues to suck, my fingers tease the wet flesh between her legs. I rub up and down, applying just enough pressure to drive her insane.

She moans against me when I slip two fingers in her tight channel. She's so wet it makes it easy to find that perfect sweet spot.

She pushes back against my hand, desperate for more contact. Giving her exactly what she craves, I reposition her once more—this time, lowering her onto my face.

Diving in, I lick her pussy like I'm never going to get the chance again.

She moans louder as my tongue delves into her folds. Grabbing her hips, I push my mouth further, driving her insane.

My dick feels amazing because she hasn't stopped sucking, but I'm entirely consumed with making her feel good. I continue to drive her crazy until I feel her coming in my mouth. She's sweet and tangy as I lap up all her juices.

She's barely come down off her orgasm before lifting herself off my face and moving down my body. Her pussy slides down my dick. She's facing away from me, still giving me a perfect view of her ass. She bounces up and down, riding me like she's a motherfucking cowgirl.

My hands rest on her hips, but I continue to let her set the pace. She alternates between sitting up and riding me fast and leaning forward and letting me slide in and out at a much slower pace. The view I have when she does that is enough to make me lose my mind. I have the perfect angle to see my dick moving in and out of her wet heat.

When she sits back up, my hands guide her hips to go harder and faster. Her hair falls down her shoulders as she throws her head back, and it's not long before we are finding our release together.

She giggles when I give her ass a light smack.

"Baby girl, I'm never letting you go."

# Chapter Thirty

## TRACY

*fifteen years ago…*

"Miss Kennedy, you need to come with me." the principal is standing in the doorway to my classroom.

Nervously, I stand up and begin to walk toward the door. I have no idea what this could be about. I haven't done anything that would get me in trouble.

At least nothing they would know about.

"Grab your things, Miss Kennedy. You won't be back today," the principal says before turning toward the teacher. "Can you please get any work for the next few days together and get it to me whenever you get the chance?"

"I won't be here for a couple of days?" I softly ask.

Instead of answering, he just says, "Please just come with me, Miss Kennedy."

My eyes look across the room at Jessie. His face shows just as much worry as I'm feeling.

Once we are out of the classroom, the old balding man stays silent.

"Mr. Ashbrook, can you tell me what this is about?" I ask.

"I'm afraid I don't know many details. I just got a call from Chief Wallace."

The chief of police? What the heck is going on?

I don't entirely believe Mr. Ashbrook when he says he

doesn't know anything, but I decide not to push the issue. The man already doesn't seem to like me much.

As promised, Chief Wallace is waiting outside with his patrol car. He opens the door for me, and I climb into the backseat. I'm about to ask him what's going on, but his phone rings. When he answers, I'm guessing it's his wife from the way he's talking.

He's driving painstakingly slow—or maybe it just feels that way.

When my house finally comes into view, I see more police cars along with an ambulance and fire truck.

My heart thumps in my chest as I try to open the door before the car has even stopped. I'm frustrated when the door won't open—stupid cop cars.

The chief puts it in park and hurries over to open the door for me. The second the fresh air hits me, I take off like a bullet shot out of a gun. My feet carry me as fast as they can toward the crowd of people that's gathered in front of the door.

I'm barreling through all of them. I'm almost through when I feel my body being lifted off the ground. The smell of my dad's cologne hits me as I feel his big arms engulf me in a hug.

"Tracy," he says with a sniffle. "Something awful has happened."

Without any warning, tears sting my eyes. He doesn't have to say what happened because as he's carrying me away, I see the sight that will forever haunt me.

Two hands pulling a sheet over my dead momma's face.

\*\*\*\*\*\*\*\*\*\*\*\*\*\*\*\*\*\*\*\*\*\*\*\*\*\*\*\*\*\*\*\*\*\*\*\*\*\*\*\*\*\*\*\*\*\*\*\*\*\*\*\*\*\*\*\*

A few days later, the funeral is coming to a close. People got up and spoke about how great my momma was, but I don't think I heard a single word any of them said.

That first day, I cried so hard I didn't think I'd ever stop. Since then, I just feel numb. Nothing has been fun. All I do is eat, sleep, and mindlessly flip through channels for hours on end.

The only thing I've wanted to do is go see Jessie, but my dad won't let me out of his sight. He says we need to spend time as a family.

It's just him and me now—it doesn't feel like much of a family.

Now, I'm at this funeral watching everyone apologize to my daddy and say their goodbyes to my momma. I don't know why I still have to be here. I wiggle in my chair from this itchy dress and these uncomfortable shoes.

When the service is over, and they're about to close the casket, my daddy says, "Why don't you go see her?"

I shake my head.

"Trace, you haven't gone within ten feet of the casket this whole time."

*There's a reason for that.*

He grabs my hand. "Come on. I'll go up with you."

This time, I shake my head more vigorously. "I don't want to."

I fight against him, but it's no use. My father is a giant compared to me. When we get to the big wooden box, I take one final look.

She looks beautiful with her long auburn hair that they've braided and draped over her shoulder. Freckles line her cheeks and the bridge of her nose. Her eyes are closed, but I can picture her green eyes. It's almost like looking in a mirror at what I will look like in twenty years.

I wonder if I'll be as beautiful as she was.

Tears begin to fill my own eyes once again, and I can't take any more.

Shrugging out of my father's grip, I spring for the door, pushing past all the people in my way.

I hear my dad say, "Let her go," as I fling open the door. Once I'm outside, I kick off those stupid shoes and take off running toward the woods.

In my itchy black dress, I run all the way to the lake—Jessie and my secret spot. It's the only place in the world that has any chance at making me feel better.

I take a seat by the water's edge and skip some stones along the surface. The only sounds are the plunking of the rocks and the birds chirping. It's much more peaceful than the constant drone of the voices at the funeral. I just couldn't take it anymore.

Looking around at the pure beauty of this place makes me sad that I never brought my momma here. I was so concerned with keeping this place a secret that I never even considered showing it to her.

And now I'll never get to.

She would have loved it. She was always able to appreciate the beauty in nature.

The past few days, I've been aware that my momma's dead, but it's just now starting to sink in that I'll never see her again. Every time a memory of her pops into my head, I get sad because I realize we will never make another memory like that again.

I wipe a single tear from my cheek, hoping that no more of them fall.

When I hear footsteps behind me, I don't have to turn around to see who it is.

*Jessie.*

"Hey, T," he says.

I don't say anything, so he just takes a seat next to me. "Momma and I went to say our goodbyes, but your daddy said you'd just run off. I knew exactly where you'd be."

"I just couldn't be there anymore. It was too dang hard."

"I don't blame you. Funerals suck."

We are both quiet for a minute as if neither of us knows what to say.

Finally, he says, "Where did your shoes go?" He looks down at my feet that are now covered in dirt and grass.

"I don't know. I kicked them off while I was running."

"You really have to stop losing shoes, or your daddy is going to kill you."

I don't say anything, but I know he's right. I have a bad habit of leaving my shoes in the middle of the woods and never seeing them again. Who cares? I don't need shoes anyway. I'd rather be barefoot.

When I'm still quiet, he says, "You know I've been trying to call you all week. I even came by once, but your daddy said you weren't up for talking."

I roll my eyes. "I think that was *him* that wasn't up for company. He hasn't let me out of his sight. He's turned our house into a jail."

"That sucks," he says, picking at his nails.

"No joke. And it wouldn't be so bad, but it's not like either of us are talking. He's barely spoken a single word since she died."

Jessie doesn't say anything, so I go on.

"Do you think it will always be like this? My daddy and me like a couple of zombies, just going through the motions, trying to pretend that everything's okay?"

He holds up one finger. "First of all, T, if you *were* a zombie, I'd take you out. So, don't you worry about that."

I can't help but laugh as he mimics getting a headshot on me.

*Maybe we've watched too many zombie movies lately.*

"And second, I'm sure things will get better. It will probably just take a little time."

"How much time?" I ask.

His shoulders shrug. "I wish I knew. But I know that I'll be right here with you for as long as you need—even if you are practically a zombie."

That *is* one thing I'm sure of. Jessie has always been by my side, and I don't see that ever changing.

He stands up and reaches for my hand. "Come on, T. Momma gave me some money, and I'll buy you an ice cream."

Grabbing his hand, I stand up and we start to walk back toward town, holding hands the entire way.

He looks down at my dirty feet, "And maybe on the way, we can try to find your shoes."

# Chapter Thirty-one

## TRACY

The following day, I jolt myself awake out of my dream. I dreamed about my mom's death. I used to dream about it all the time, but it's been years since the last time. Apparently, this trip has jarred some of those memories loose.

My heart races as I try to calm myself down. Suddenly, I feel an arm wrap around me, pulling me closer. When I realize it's Jessie, my body instinctively begins to relax.

I flip around, so I'm facing him. I push a strand of his dark brown hair out of his face and then take a moment to look at him.

Jessie has always been handsome. When we were kids, people would always say he would grow up and be a heart-breaker. And when we were teenagers, girls would always talk about how cute he was and flirt with him.

Now that we are older, he's even more handsome. He finally grew a little bit of facial hair—and some chest hair.

My fingertips run across the stubble along his jaw. I stop, taking the time to feel the slight indent on the right side of his chin. I remember when he fell off his bike and cracked his chin on a rock. The stitches led to a tiny scar. I was with him when it happened and used my sweatshirt to try to stop the bleeding.

It's crazy how much we know about each other, yet now we are trying to fill in the blanks from the past few years. To be honest, I don't care about what happened in the time we were apart. We both had lives that we lived apart. Now, we are putting those lives together.

And I'd say this trip seems like an excellent start. This whole week has been a good start. And right now, this moment seems perfect.

I've never been one to care if I have someone sleeping next to me. Sleeping alone doesn't bother me. On the contrary, I've always enjoyed my alone time.

Yet, I find myself wanting to give up that alone time to be with Jessie. I enjoy sleeping next to him. He makes me feel safe—and that's saying a lot when I'm a girl who sleeps with a shotgun in her closet.

"T, what are you doing?" Jessie mumbles, causing me to jump.

"What do you mean?"

"You're staring at me."

"How do you know that? Your eyes are closed."

"I can feel your eyes."

I run my finger over his bottom lip. "Maybe I think you're cute."

"Oh, yeah?"

"Mm-hmm." I pause. "Even with the morning breath."

He smiles. "Is that right? Anyone ever told you that you've got a smart mouth?"

"Oh, all the time," I joke.

Without warning, he rolls over, pinning me underneath him. "Maybe it's time someone taught you a lesson," he whispers.

"You can try," I taunt.

Pushing my arms up so they're above my head, he leans down to suck on my nipples. I yelp when I feel his teeth gently sink into the tender flesh.

I squirm underneath him, my pussy desperate for contact. Thankfully, Jessie doesn't make me wait long before sliding into me. I seem to like it when he takes charge because I'm already wet as hell.

His hands continue to hold mine in place while he slams in and out of me. It's hard and rough, and I fucking love it.

My moans get louder, and I'm sure our neighbors in the hotel can hear me. But fuck it, I don't care.

Every time he pushes into me, he grinds against my clit, bringing me closer to orgasm with every stroke.

"Jessie!" I scream out when I fly over the edge.

He moves even harder and faster while I ride the waves of pleasure washing over my body.

"Fuuuuck," he moans as he comes inside me.

When his body stills, he leans down and says in a low voice, "You seemed to like me taking charge."

I laugh. "Don't get excited, wild child. If you try that anywhere besides the bedroom, I'll kick your ass."

**********************************************************

After our morning romp in the sheets, Jessie and I get back on the road. He says he's got a plan but won't tell me where we're going. So, we ride in a comfortable silence between us—the only sound is the lull of country music on the radio.

Pretty soon, I doze off and don't wake up until I feel Jessie gently shaking me.

"Hey, T, come on. We have to walk from here."

Opening my eyes, I try to process my surroundings. It looks like we are parked in a small lot that is the start of a walking trail.

He walks around to open my door for me. When I step out, I take a moment to stretch, attempting to loosen everything up.

Taking my hand, Jessie leads me onto the trail, and we walk through the brush for a few minutes before coming to a clearing.

When we step out of the trees, I gasp. We have a first-class, panoramic view of the Smokey Mountains. For miles and miles, all we can see are hills lined with lush, green trees.

Talk about a view that makes you appreciate how beautiful the Earth really is.

"Wow," I whisper. "Beautiful."

"I remember you told me you used to come to the mountains with your parents before…"

I look over at him. "It's okay, Jessie. You can say it. Before my mom died."

He gives a weak smile. "Do you think she'd like this view?"

My lip quivers, trying to hold back my oncoming tears. "Oh, yeah. She'd love it. I could see her just wanting to sit up here for hours," I pause for a moment before adding, "I dreamed about her last night."

"What about?"

"About the day that she died. It was like I was reliving it or something. Do you remember that day?" I ask him.

"Of course. I don't think I'll ever forget it."

My fingers find his, and I hold his hand. "You were always there for me. Back then and now. You've always had a way of bringing me down to Earth when I was close to flying away."

"I wasn't there for a while, T. I walked away from the one who was in my corner no matter what. But I can promise you that I'll never make that mistake again. I've known for damn near twenty years now that you were the girl for me. I'm just sorry it took me so long to get my head out of my ass and do something about it."

I look up at him. "You're here now. Let's just move forward."

Grabbing my face, he gives me a tender kiss.

When he pulls back, I say, "Thank you for asking me to come on this trip. It's been nice getting out of Grady. Maybe it wouldn't be bad to do it a bit more often."

"Deal. But as long as I'm with you, I don't care where we are—even that crazy town of ours. Speaking of which, I'm ready to go home whenever you are. Just say the word."

I wrap my arms around him, hugging him tightly. "Let's just stay a little while longer."

# Chapter Thirty-two

## JESSIE

Our trip away ended up spanning another night. We stayed on that lookout point for hours, talking and laughing. By the time we left, we didn't want to drive all the way back, so we stopped and stayed at a hotel for one more night.

When we finally got home yesterday, we spent the day not doing much of anything—except each other. I swear Tracy is insatiable and probably loves sex just as much as I do—if not more. I'm one lucky son of a bitch.

Today, however, I don't feel all that lucky. Not because of Tracy. But because it's my first day working on the ranch, and Jonas has been kicking my ass all over the place. Don't get me wrong, I'm in good shape, and I try to stay active, but I had no idea everything that the workers do on a daily basis. Now, I see why Jonas is as strong as an ox.

We work through the day, spending time taking care of the cattle, hauling hay all over the place, and cleaning up all of the inevitable messes.

When Jonas walks away to talk to his right-hand man, Taylor, he tells me to take a break.

Plopping down to sit on a bale of hay, I pull out my phone and see I have a missed text from Tracy—from two hours ago. I must have not even felt it vibrate in my pocket.

**T: Hey, sweets. I hope you are having a good first day! How are things going?**

I quickly type out a reply.

**Me: Hey, baby girl. It's going alright. Jonas is keeping me busy, and my body isn't happy about it.**

Three tiny dots appear as she types, and I hope she responds before Jonas The Dictator comes back. Thankfully, her response is almost instant.

**T: Come over after work? I'll cook dinner and make you feel all better.**

**Me: Can't wait.**

**T: Love you, sweets. See you soon.**

I type out my response telling her I love her too, the whole time, never being able to stop smiling.

"I know that smile." Jonas comes walking back toward me. "You just got done talking to your woman. I still get that big ol' dumb smile every time I talk to Andi."

"You think you'll ever stop?" I ask.

He chuckles. "Not 'til the day I die. And even then, they'll probably toss me into the ground with that big cheesy grin on my face."

I laugh. "You and me both, Joe."

The rest of the afternoon flies by as he continues to show me the different jobs about the ranch.

When it's finally quitting time, I decide to run by my house real quick and shower. I smell like—well, a cattle ranch.

The hot water feels good on my sore muscles, but I still try not to take my time. I want to get to my woman.

Once I'm out and dry, I throw on a t-shirt and sweatpants and get ready to leave.

When my phone rings, I don't bother to look at the screen, figuring it's Tracy wondering where I'm at.

"Hey, baby girl, I'm on my way out the door," I say, looking around for where I put my keys.

But the voice I hear isn't Tracy's. Instead, it's one that stops me dead in my tracks.

"Well, that's a fun new nickname."

*Gabby.*

Gritting my teeth, I ask, "Gabby, how'd you get this number?"

When I moved back to Grady, I got a new phone with a new number—for a fresh start and all that.

"I have my ways," she says, trying to play coy.

"Doesn't matter," I mumble. "What the hell do you want?"

"I want to see you. I'm doing a lot better, and I was hoping we could talk about it. I miss you, baby."

Every word she speaks makes bile rise in my throat. Gabby is everything in my life that I am desperate to forget.

Instinctively, my eyes dart over to the box that holds that old sonogram photo, and my heart hurts for our baby that could have been—our baby that *should* have been.

"Gabby, I don't want to do this with you. When I left, I made it very clear that we were over. That hasn't changed."

"But what we had was good. I miss it, baby," she says, using her pouty voice.

"Gabby, I'm not your baby. You and I are through. I've moved on, and you should too."

"You found someone else?" She asks.

"It's none of your business, Gabby. Now, lose my number," I command as I click off the phone.

Knowing she won't listen, I pull up her number and block it. I don't want to hear from that woman ever again.

Storming out of the house, I get in my truck and take off. I decide to take the long way to Tracy's in hopes that I calm down before I get there.

She and I are doing so great. I don't want this Gabby thing to jeopardize it.

My mind races with thoughts of Gabby. It's crazy how the idea of her used to get me so excited. Now, it just gives me a massive pit in my gut.

The first night Gabby ever walked into a bar I worked at, she caught my attention right away. I was instantly drawn to her wild, carefree personality. Maybe a part of me thought she'd be a little like Tracy—a gorgeous wildflower.

It didn't take long to realize that Gabby's wild ways were self-destructive—the exact opposite of Tracy's.

It was fun for a while, but I quickly learned that the fun was only present when we were both high. Whenever I was sober, I could see how unstable she was—and how dangerous we were as a couple. That's probably why she'd used all of her trust fund money to keep us flying high. Every time I tried to talk to her about any of our issues, she'd suggest we'd have some fun and then talk about it.

Spoiler alert: we'd never get around to talking about it.

Not until after we lost the baby anyway. Then, she'd make promises day in and day out about she'd get clean, but then, I'd catch her using once more.

I understand relapse. I've been through it plenty of times, but when she outright told me she had no intention of quitting and all her promises were lies she told to keep me around, I knew we were done. And seeing her sucking her dealer's cock cemented that fact.

The really fucked up thing was that she was so high that she didn't even apologize when I caught her. I didn't hear from her until I was halfway out of town. I talked to her one final time to tell her things were over. She was sober at the time and seemed to understand.

So, I have no idea why the fuck she's calling me now. That door is shut, and I sure as hell don't want to ever open it again.

Shaking my head, I do my best to shake out any and all thoughts of Gabby and my past mistakes right out of my brain. I'm not letting that phone call ruin my night with Tracy.

I consider whether or not I'm going to tell her about this incident and ultimately decide that I'm just going to play it by ear.

Finally, I pull into her driveway. The gravel crunches under my tires before I put the truck in park. Then, taking a deep breath, I step out and head inside.

When I step through the front door, the lights are all on low, creating a warm glow all around the room. And candles are burning on each of the tables. Country music is playing through some small speakers. It's not loud—just enough to add a little background noise.

Walking through the living room, I call for Tracy but get no response. Finally, when I get to the kitchen, I see her standing out back by her small grill.

I take a moment to just look at her. Her wild, wavy auburn hair is gently blowing in the wind. Her clean, white tank top brings out the color of her tan.

My eyes wander down to her cut-off jean shorts, which hug her ample ass and thick thighs. She's standing barefoot in the grass, sipping on a can of beer.

Damn, she's beautiful—beautiful in a way that she doesn't even realize. Tracy Kennedy has that natural beauty that you hope and pray your future wife has. I hope one day, I'll get the chance to call her my wife. I don't know if I'll ever be truly good enough for her, though. I don't know that I'll ever deserve her—especially if my past keeps coming to call.

*Stop it. You're not going to let anything ruin this night.*

Something seems to catch her attention, and she turns her head to look inside the sliding glass door. Quickly, I walk toward her, trying to act like I wasn't just staring like a weirdo.

"Hey," she greets me with a warm smile. "I didn't know you were on your way. I was trying to have dinner ready."

"I'm sorry, baby girl. I should've texted. Just a little trapped in my head, I guess."

Her hand rubs my shoulder. "You okay?"

Once again, I consider telling her what happened but decide that tonight isn't the time. "I'm good. Just tired. Jonas kicked my ass today, showing me the ropes."

There's a look in her eye that shows she doesn't entirely believe me, and I wait for her to call me on my bullshit. But she doesn't. Instead, she stands on her tip-toes, leans close, and kisses me on the cheek.

"I'm sorry, sweets. I'll try to make you feel better tonight."

I smile. "Just seeing you makes me feel better."

She rolls her eyes. "Such a charmer."

Turning around, she goes to step away from me, but my hand grasps her arm, pulling her back. I grab her chin between my thumb and finger, angling her face up toward mine.

"Just because I'm a charmer doesn't mean I don't mean every single word."

She tries not to smile, but she's not doing a very good job. "Well played, wild child. Well played."

She walks back inside the house to grab a clean plate for the steaks she's just grilled. I've never met anyone who loves red meat as much as Tracy, and that's saying a lot coming from someone who now works on a cattle ranch.

I try to help, but she insists that I sit down and relax. When I go to argue, she gives me a glare that could shoot daggers, so I sit down and shut up.

Five minutes later, two plates sit in front of us with rib-eye steaks, corn on the cob, and rolls.

When I cut into my steak and take a bite, the meat practically melts in my mouth, and it's seasoned perfectly. I hate to admit it, but this woman's skills on the grill far surpass my own.

"Damn, baby girl. This is amazing," I say between bites.

She smiles. "Glad you like it."

"Where did you learn to grill a steak like this?"

"Practice. I mean, my dad taught me the basics, but I tweaked my methods over the years. Now, Daddy has handed over all grilling duties to me."

"I can see why." I sip my water before asking. "How was your day?"

"It was okay. I had almost all of the staff working, so I was able to get some paperwork done in the back."

"It sounds like a good thing, but your tone says otherwise."

She picks at her roll. "Well, it's good to get stuff done, but I prefer being out on the floor—helping customers and all that.

That's why I try to save most of the paperwork for just one day a week."

Tracy Kennedy always keeps me on my toes. While at work, she seems to be an extrovert—interacting with everyone and loving it. But when it comes to anything too personal, she plays things close to the vest—never letting anyone get too close except me. Somehow, I've always been lucky enough to be welcomed into her tight-knit world.

We talk more about our days until both of us finish eating. Then, I help her clean up by loading the dishwasher.

Once we are done, she pulls me close, reaching her hands under my shirt and lightly rubbing my stomach. I can smell the citrus scent of her soap and the coconut smell of her shampoo. She smells like a damn tropical paradise.

"Come on, sweets. Let's go to bed, and I'll rub you all over," She says with a sultry smile. "Unless you're too sore."

Scooping her up and over my shoulder, I smack her ass before heading into the bedroom.

Suddenly, I don't feel sore at all.

# Chapter Thirty-three

## TRACY

Something isn't right. Ever since Jessie came over last night, he's been off. Despite him swearing up and down that he's just tired, it seems like more than that. I'm just not sure what.

Maybe he's regretting taking that job with Jonas. That would fit since it was his first day working on the ranch. Maybe he didn't realize exactly what he was getting into, and now he's wishing he would have stayed working at the bar.

Once we went to the bedroom last night, the sex was good —mind-blowing, as usual. But when we went to sleep, he tossed and turned most of the night. Usually, the man sleeps like a log, so I notice when he's moving around more than usual.

This morning, he kissed me, told me he loved me, and we both headed off to work. To most, everything would seem normal. But I just have a weird feeling that I can't seem to shake.

However, unlike everyone in this town, I'm going to give him the benefit of the doubt.

So, I will believe him when he tells me nothing is wrong.

For now.

And I'm going to keep myself busy at work today in order to avoid thinking about all of it. And it's almost working.

Almost.

I'm about to drive myself crazy when I get a text from

Andi to see if I want to do lunch. Thank goodness because I'm starving.

We meet over at a diner that is only a few doors down from my shop. It has some of the best food within a hundred miles—that delicious, down-home comfort food.

Andi is already there waiting for me when I arrive. I slide into the booth across from her, and there are already two sodas sitting on the table.

"I took the liberty of ordering you a Coke," she says, taking a sip of her own.

"You know me so well."

"Well, I didn't order you any food yet. I wasn't sure what your garbage disposal of a stomach would be in the mood for today."

Sticking my nose in the air, I try to figure out what the woman at the table behind me is eating because it smells phenomenal. Finally, after a few sniffs, I decide.

"Meatloaf," I tell our waitress, Suzie when she comes to check on us. "Meatloaf, mashed potatoes, mac and cheese, and green beans, please."

Andi orders some of the fried chicken, and we hand our menus back to Suzie.

My friend shakes her head at me. "I don't know how you eat like that. If I ate as much as you do, my ass would be as big as a dump truck. Hell, I'm just about there now."

I wave her off. "You're gorgeous, and you know it. Besides, I have a butt too. The problem is that it looks a little disproportionate on me because I don't have the big boobs to balance out."

She looks down at her ample chest. "I guess I have those too. You're welcome to take some of mine."

"If only," I croon. "How are the boys doing?"

"They're good. Not quite as many nightmares lately, which is nice. Jonas and I are looking into actually adopting them."

I grin. "That's awesome! I'm happy for you guys. How's that going to go over with the boys' dad?"

Andi told me that the boys' mom died a few years back, and their dad just recently got into some legal trouble, hence why they ended up in foster care.

She pushes her springy black curls out of her eyes. "His trial was last week. For all of his counts of fraud, he won't be getting out of prison until he's a very, very old man. I guess the judge had a talk with him about how maybe it would be best for his kids if he signed his rights over. Thankfully, it didn't take much convincing. So, now we just have to file the paperwork, pass all of the home checks, and all that. Then, it's just a waiting game.

"Whoa," I say. "Two kids. You ready to handle that for the rest of your life?"

Her fingers fiddle with her straw wrapper, and she smiles. "I'm more ready than I've ever been for anything. And it helps that I have a partner who is pretty damn near perfect. I couldn't ask for anyone better to have by my side."

"That's awesome," I say before taking another drink.

"You ever think about having kids?"

She asks the question, and it takes me completely off guard. I start choking on my drink, and it burns as some of the soda gets into my nose.

"Don't surprise me like that!" I say between coughs.

"Trace, we were talking about kids. I don't think it's that big of a jump to ask you about your plans."

"I don't have any plans."

"You don't want kids?"

I take a deep breath because, truth be told, I have no idea what I want. "I don't know, Andi. Kids are alright. I mean, I haven't been around them much, but I wouldn't mind having them someday. The problem is that I run a business that takes up a lot of time. I don't think I'm ready to give that up any time soon."

"You know, the two things don't have to be mutually exclusive."

"In my experience, they do especially with men in these

small towns. They all think that a woman should be a mom first...that a woman should be a mom *only.* They all seem to think that she should stay home once a woman becomes a wife and a mom. I just don't know that I'm ready to do that."

"Do you think someone like Jessie would have that mindset?" She asks.

"Hell, I don't know, Andi. We haven't even come remotely close to talking about any of that. But I mean, Jessie's mom was a stay-at-home mother, and that woman deserves to win an award for her motherhood skills. I have to imagine that Jessie would want the same for his own kids."

Thankfully, our food shows up, giving me a reason to change the subject. After I comment on the food, Andi adds, "Just don't presume to know what Jessie wants before you actually ask him."

I agree, but I have no intention of asking Jessie about all of that any time soon. We are just getting started again—no need to rush things.

While we eat, I keep the conversation focused on her life, asking her questions about Jonas and the kids. She seems thrilled to talk about it, and it keeps the glare of the spotlight off me for a little while.

Once we are done eating, Andi walks me back toward the shop, and we are about to say our goodbyes when Marlow waves us down. We stop walking, and the nosy woman comes shuffling across the street.

"Lord, here we go," Andi mumbles under her breath.

"Tracy, dear. I just wanted to come to check on you," Marlow says, almost out of breath.

"Why would you need to check on me?"

"The other night, I saw the Mitchell boy and you get into it. You ran outside, pointing a shotgun at him. I was going to call the police, but you seemed to have it under control." Her tone tries to be sympathetic, but it comes off much more condescending.

Andi's eyes are wide at hearing that I pointed a gun at her

brother-in-law.

"Marlow, I'm fine. I had forgotten Jessie said he was coming over, and he startled me, is all." Maybe it's a little bit of a lie, but I'm not giving her any more ammunition to hate Jessie.

But my plan doesn't work because she starts in anyway. "I don't know what you're doing with that boy. He's nothing but trouble, and you can do so much better."

I begin to open my mouth, but she keeps on, "Are you just attracted to the bad boys? Is that what it is? Or does he have some sort of leverage over you? I can't imagine any other reason you would stick around. He's a no-good loser who is just as bad as his no-good daddy of his. He's going to drag you down that awful road right along with him."

"Marlow," I practically spit. "Leave us alone. You don't know a thing about Jessie or a thing about me. Stop acting like you have any idea what goes on in our relationship."

"I'm just trying to help, dear."

"No, you're not. You're trying to be nosy and stick your big nose where it doesn't belong. Jessie is good, and if you had even a speck of compassion, you would ask him how he's doing, and maybe you'd realize how entirely wrong you are. But heaven forbid you do that because you might actually have to admit that you were wrong." My blood boils as my voice gets louder. "So, you and Brenda can take your snide comments and your worthless opinions and shove them up your asses."

Marlow's hand covers her heart as though she can't imagine how anyone could speak to her like that. Her mouth gapes at my words, but before she can respond, I grab Andi's hand and lead her away.

Once we are inside the store, she says, "That was pretty bad-ass. Next time, you should punch her. I'd like to see that."

"Don't tempt me," I groan.

"That woman will just never learn. Between her and Brenda, they're determined to run Jessie and me right out of town." Andi spits.

"Screw them," I say. "They just aren't happy with their

own lives, so they feel the need to try to ruin everyone else's."

My phone vibrates in my pocket, and when I see it's Jessie who texted, I immediately smile, but when I read his message, it quickly fades.

**Jessie: Hey baby girl, I have to run to Nashville this evening, so I probably won't see you until tomorrow sometime. I have to handle something, and I promise I'll explain everything when I get back. I love you.**

Okay, maybe I spoke too soon about how Jessie has changed.

# Chapter Thirty-four

## JESSIE

*What the fuck am I doing?*

My old truck flies down the highway in the direction of all the signs that point to Nashville.

The phone calls from Gabby haven't stopped. Every time I block a number, she calls or texts me from a different one. She insists that we should talk, and she doesn't want to take no for an answer.

When she sent me a text threatening to show up in Grady, I decided to go to her. Maybe when she sees the look on my face, she can see that I'm serious about our relationship being over.

Guilt eats away at me because I didn't tell Tracy what was going on. I just told her I had to go to Nashville. When I said I loved her, all I got in response was a "see you tomorrow." I don't blame her, though. I'd be pissed with me too.

I considered going by the store and talking to her before I left, but if I want to make it to Nashville and back before morning, I needed to leave right after I got off work. I explained to Jonas a little of what was going on, and he told me I could take extra time if I needed to, but I'm trying to do this whole 'responsible adult' thing, which means not missing a ton of work during my first week.

I'll just be tired as shit tomorrow. But if I can get Gabby out of my life for good, it will be completely worth it. I'll lose sleep for that any day of the week.

My stomach is a wreck, and I feel like I'm going to throw up at any moment. This whole walking a tight rope between escaping my past while not throwing away my future is going to give me an ulcer.

The truck is silent around me. The only sound audible is my tires running over the asphalt and my occasional sigh. This is going to be the longest drive of my life.

\*\*\*\*\*\*\*\*\*\*\*\*\*\*\*\*\*\*\*\*\*\*\*\*\*\*\*\*\*\*\*\*\*\*\*\*\*\*\*\*\*\*\*\*\*\*\*\*\*\*\*\*\*\*\*\*\*

When I pull up to Gabby's apartment, my fingers clench the steering wheel so hard that my knuckles are turning white. I passed the time by reflecting on all the bad memories I have of being here in Nashville. A ball of white-hot rage replaces the uneasy pit in my gut.

When I stopped to gas up the truck, I texted Tracy to check in, but she hasn't answered me. I try to tell myself that she's just busy, but I know she's probably pissed. I left her with a lot of questions when I left, and now, she's more than happy to return the favor.

It occurs to me that it would be all too easy to lose a woman like Tracy, so I'm going to make this visit the end of my dealings with Gabby.

Stepping out of the truck, I slam the door and make my way up to the second floor.

When Gabby opens the door, it isn't quite the Gabby that I remember. She certainly looks more put-together than she used to. Her long blonde hair hangs almost to her ass now, and she has side bangs that show off her face, which doesn't look nearly as gaunt as it used to.

"Jessie," she smiles. "I've missed you."

She swings open the door and wraps her arms around my neck, but I peel them off the moment they touch me.

"Gabby, you wanted to talk. I'm here. Talk."

Her tongue runs over her bottom lip. "Look at you...being all alpha. You know I used to love when you'd take charge."

"I don't think you'll like it so much anymore," I spit.

"Don't be so sure about that. Remember when you used to handcuff me to the bed?"

"Enough, Gabby! Why am I here?"

Walking over to the couch, she sits down and gestures for me to sit in the chair across from her. I follow her but stay standing.

The apartment is a lot nicer than it used to be too. Nicer furniture, and it's cleaner than it ever was when I lived here. My first thought is I wonder who she had to sleep with to get all these nice things. It sounds awful of me, but maybe some old wounds of mine aren't healed yet.

"Jessie," her soft voice pulls me from my thoughts. "Ever since you left, I've been working on getting my life in order. You told me that you couldn't be with someone so careless with her life…and the lives of those around her. I took that to heart, and I've been working hard to be someone worthy of your love.

"When you left, and the fog lifted, I was devastated. I thought about coming after you, but I knew I would need to have something good to say. I'd need to have something good to *show* you. So, I got clean. It took a while, and I had many stints of slipping back down the slope, but I've been sober for four months now. I found a new job that I love, and I don't want to live my life any longer without you, J."

Her words sound great. Lord knows, I waited for months and months to hear them. But anything that Gabby and I had is in the past.

"Look, Gabby, I'm happy you got your life in order. Really, I am. You look great, and the apartment looks great, but all of this is just too little too late."

Her face falls. "You met someone…"

She says it as more of a statement than a question.

"More like someone and I found our way back to each other after far too long."

"That girl who used to be your best friend?"

I'm a little taken back at her question because I don't remember ever talking to her about Tracy.

She sees the confusion on my face and says, "You talked about her one night when you were pretty drunk. You told me how she broke your heart."

I give in and take a seat in the chair across from her. "More like we broke each other's hearts."

She leans back on the couch. "Tell me about her."

"Tracy is just…Tracy. I don't even know how to describe her, except she's the woman of my dreams. I've known that since we were five years old. I thought getting out of Grady would change that, but the moment I saw her again, I just knew."

I feel bad that I'm gushing about my current girlfriend to my ex, so I try to reel it back and stop talking, but Gabby seems genuinely interested to learn more.

"You sound happy, J," she says.

"I am. And I'm sorry, Gabby, but I'm not willing to give that up. I'm glad you're doing so well, but you deserve someone who will love you the way you deserve."

"Like the way you love her?"

"Yeah. Like the way I love her."

I was thinking about how I would give her hell the entire drive up here, but she seems to be handling this far better than I imagined she would. Something feels off, but I'm not about to look a gift horse in the mouth.

"I'm sorry you came all the way out here," she says. "I thought that you just didn't want to talk to me because you thought everything was how it used to be. I thought if maybe you saw me, you'd think maybe we could have a second chance."

"I'm sorry, Gabby. It's just not going to happen."

"Maybe we can stay friends?" She gives a weak smile.

Now, I'm about to hurt her feelings even more. "I don't know if that's a good idea either."

"Ah. So, the new girl is jealous?"

I chuckle. "A little, but it's more than that. When I left Nashville, I left behind some old habits and bad memories. I've worked hard to stay away from them and start over. That becomes a whole lot harder to do if you and I stay friends."

Disappointment is written on her face, but she tries not to show it. "I get it."

"For what it's worth, though, I am proud of you. You did a great job at getting your life back on track."

She smiles. "Thank you. It's been tough, but I did it. And I don't plan on going back."

"Good to hear." I glance at my phone, taking note of the time.

"Do you need to get going?" She asks.

"Yeah, probably. It's a long drive back to Grady, and I have to work in the morning."

"Where are you working now?"

Standing up, I reply, "My brother's cattle ranch. He gave me a job and is letting me stay in his guest house for a while."

"That's awesome, J. I'm happy for you."

She stands up to hug me goodbye, and I take one final look at Gabby and the apartment we used to share. I take one last look at the life we used to have. I feel like I should feel sad about it or something, but honestly, I'm just excited about walking away and never looking back.

Once I'm out of the apartment, I practically sprint back to my truck, excited to get home to Tracy. But when I get driving and calculate the time it'll take to get back, I realize it will be way too late to go Tracy's—or way too *early,* I should say.

She might bring out that shotgun again but this time, actually shoot me. I still haven't heard anything back from her, so I assume she is pretty pissed. I don't blame her. I'd be pissed too. But, hopefully, this is the last time I even come close to hurting her.

I decide that tomorrow, after work, I will go and grovel and beg for her forgiveness. I pray she understands, and we can put this whole mess behind us.

I get back on the highway, heading back home. This time, I crank the music up and step on the gas, leaving Nashville and my sordid past in the rearview mirror.

# Chapter Thirty-five

## TRACY

The following day, I'm not scheduled to work since I have a meeting with a local designer. When the meeting takes far less time than I thought it would, I decide to go fishing for the day to clear my mind.

Jessie has texted me a couple of times, but I haven't answered him. I'm not exactly thrilled about how he handled things yesterday, and he still has given me absolutely no details on what the hell happened to make him run off to Nashville.

Deciding to try to make amends with my dad, I invite him to come along. It doesn't take too much convincing. After I pick him up, we drive to a lake about twenty miles away. It's not nearly as pretty as the secret spot Jessie and I share, but it's big, has a nice dock for fishing, and is usually pretty well stocked.

When we are finally situated with our baited poles in the water, I lean my head back and close my eyes.

But when my dad's gruff voice begins to speak, it pulls me out of my thoughts. "So, why fishing?"

My eyes dart over to him and squint. "You love to fish."

He nods. "I know that."

"And I love to fish. So, what's the problem?"

"The problem is that it is noon on a weekday. So you're usually at the shop or doing something that pertains to the shop."

"I had a meeting this morning, but it ended early, so I decided just to relax the rest of the day."

He makes a noise that's somewhere between a scoff and a chortle. "You? Relaxing? I don't think so."

"I know how to relax," I insist.

"Tracy Kennedy, I swear to you that you've barely relaxed a single day since the day you were born. You've always been on the move, trying to conquer the world one day at a time. It seemed like the only time you stopped to breathe was when Jessie was around." The mention of Jessie's name makes me shudder a bit. I'm trying not to think about him.

He continues. "Hell, even when you were a kid, and we'd go fishing, it was like a job to you. You had to catch more fish than anyone else. And lord help us if we tried to leave before you were done. You've always been a workhorse, Trace. There's nothing wrong with that. I just worry that with all your work and all your fussing over me, you'll miss out on your life."

"Daddy, don't worry about any of that. I love my life just the way that it is. But, you know if I had too much free time on my hands, I'd probably go crazy."

He chuckles. "Probably. Have you thought about getting a hobby?"

"What the hell do you think fishing is?" I ask. "You should know. You're the one that got me hooked on it."

"That's not true, darlin'. Your momma was the one who would take you out fishing when you were little. After that, I would just tag along with the two of you. Your love for it definitely came from her."

"What?" I ask. I vaguely remember Momma coming with us on occasion, but I don't remember she and I doing a lot of it with just us.

"Trace, I was working on the farm dang near every day. Your momma was home and bored, so she would take you out on all sorts of adventures. She took you hiking when you were just barely old enough to walk. And she took you fishing not long after that. You were her little sidekick for all her adventures."

"Why don't I remember that?" My mind sorts through memories like they're in a file folder, trying to make these memories magically appear.

But I've got nothing.

"You were so little that you probably wouldn't remember. As you started getting older, your momma knew that I felt like I was missing so much. She convinced me to hire some help around the farm so that I could spend more time with the two of you. It meant money got even tighter, but looking back, I am so thankful for that time I had with the two of you." He sighs. "It was almost like your momma knew her days were numbered, and she convinced me to spend every moment possible with you two."

"She was pretty great, wasn't she?" I smile at just the thought of her.

It dawns on me that I am now just a couple of years younger than she was when she died.

"Daddy, what do you think she'd be like if she were still alive?"

"A lot like you, I suppose. Or you would be a lot like her—however you want to look at it. I swear when your momma died, she left you with part of her soul because sometimes, you are so much like her, it's insane."

I smile because I will always take that as a compliment. "She was a lot sweeter than I am. I'm a little more of an asshole."

He belly laughs. "Well, you *are* half mine, after all. You had to inherit something from me."

I nod. "Very true."

He shares a few more stories about my momma, and then he decides to change the subject. "So, how's Jessie doing? I assume you're mad at him."

"Why would you assume that?"

"Once again, you're fishing at noon on a weekday."

I shake my head. "Nope. Everything is fine. Just taking it slow is all." I don't know at what point my dad became so invested in my dating life. He's always asked questions here or there, but really, he's always just preferred I keep it short and sweet. He's never been much for all the touchy-feely stuff.

Yet here we are.

When I don't say anything else, he adds, "Just don't be too hard on the boy. It sounds like he's been through a lot."

I'm tempted to give my side of things, but I have a feeling that's his plan. Bait me to try to get me to talk.

Not today, old man.

Instead of arguing, I just say, "You know if you keep talking so much, you're going to scare all the fish away."

At that moment, he remembers I inherited another fundamental trait from him.

My stubbornness.

\*\*\*\*\*\*\*\*\*\*\*\*\*\*\*\*\*\*\*\*\*\*\*\*\*\*\*\*\*\*\*\*\*\*\*\*\*\*\*\*\*\*\*\*\*\*\*\*\*\*\*\*\*\*\*\*\*\*\*\*\*\*

Later that evening, I'm standing at my kitchen counter fileting the fish that I caught. It's not a huge haul, but I did alright.

I hear my front door swing open. Maybe I should be worried, but I'm pretty positive I know who it is. When I didn't answer his calls or texts all day, I knew Jessie would eventually just show up.

"T," he calls out.

"Kitchen," is all I respond with.

When he comes in, worry is written all over his face. "You're a hard woman to get ahold of."

"Only when you act like a dick," I quip.

"Well, I've come to grovel if you'll listen."

Without taking my eyes off the fish in front of me, I say, "Grovel away."

"Not sure I want to do that while you have a giant knife in your hand," he says with a weak laugh.

But when I glare at him, he decides maybe it's not the best time to joke.

"Something happened the other night," he begins. "On my way over here, I got a phone call...from Gabby."

"Gabby? As in your ex, Gabby?" Uneasiness washes over

me, wondering where this is going.

"Yeah, that's the one. She called saying she wanted to see me and try to start things up again."

Well, now it makes sense why he was so out of it the other night. Deciding I don't need to hear anymore, I quickly wash my hands and dry them before walking into the other room.

"Good for you," I mumble. "I hope you'll be very happy."

"Whoa, whoa, whoa!" He follows after me. "I didn't take her up on the offer. In fact, I told her that I never wanted to talk to her again. I even blocked her number, but she just kept calling from other numbers, so yesterday, I decided to drive to Nashville to talk to her in person so that she would get the message."

"How'd that go?" I ask, sitting on the couch. He sits next to me, but I take one of the throw pillows and put it between us so he can't scoot over any closer.

"It went a lot easier than I thought it would actually. She said she understood."

"She understood? Just like that?" Something smells fishy... and it's not my hands.

"I guess I portrayed to her just how in love with you I was. I told her that I found my perfect girl, and I wasn't going to let her go—no matter what."

"I'm sure she loved that," I say sarcastically.

"I don't care what she loved. Don't you get it? From now on, I'm only caring what you love. It's you and me, baby girl. And I'm sorry I didn't tell you about all of this, but I figured I could get it all taken care of without having you worry."

I cut him off. "Jessie, let me make this clear to you. If it's you and me, then you can't hide things from me. If it's your problem, it's my problem too. That's how this works. If I had a problem and didn't come to tell you about it, wouldn't you be upset? Wouldn't you want to know so that you could help? Or would you rather me just handle everything by myself?"

He pauses for a moment and thinks about my words before answering. "You're right."

"I know. I'm always right." I smile.

I'm not entirely over being mad, but I guess Jessie's explanation makes sense. I meant what I said though—we either do this as a team or not at all. I'm not some damsel that needs to be protected. I can handle myself.

"Are you still mad at me?" He asks.

"A little," I reply.

"How can I make it up to you?"

I think for a moment. "You can finish fileting those fish."

He laughs. "I'm not sure I even know how to do that. It's been years since I have attempted it."

Standing up, I walk back into the kitchen. "Come on, wild child. Time for a refresher course."

# Chapter Thirty-six

## JESSIE

"Have I told you how beautiful you are?" I ask Tracy, lying in bed next to her.

"You don't have to keep sucking up." She smiles. "You finished the fish. So I think you're off the hook...for now anyway."

"I'm not sucking up. I think you're beautiful."

My fingers trace along her collarbone, where a few freckles are scattered across the skin. "Can I kiss all of your freckles?"

She giggles. "We might be here a while. I remember when we were younger, you would ask me if you could draw on me with a marker to connect them all."

"I thought it would be fun. Almost like a connect the dots. Maybe they'd make a cool picture or something."

"And maybe I could beat you up," she jokes.

"How about this?"

Before she can ask what I am talking about, I take my tongue and lick from one freckle to the next all the way across her chest. As I go lower, tracing the tiny marks toward her breasts, her body quivers beneath me.

"I can't see the rest of your freckles. I think you should take this off," I say, tugging her tank top over her head.

Once it's off, I take my time giving attention to every one of her cute little freckles.

She moans when I pull her nipple into my mouth and swirl my tongue around the tip.

"You like that, baby girl?" I ask.

She nods frantically and moans, "More."

But I don't give it to her, opting to continue teasing her instead.

Soon enough, she can't take anymore and playfully pushes me off her and flat onto my back. She yanks my clothes off and begins lightly running her nails down my chest and stomach and stopping just before she gets to my dick.

Then, her hands move to my thighs, teasing up and down. My cock is so hard and almost twitching, begging for her to touch it. But she doesn't.

Okay, maybe I understand why the teasing thing is so frustrating because I'm about to lose my mind.

Her pussy hovers just above where I crave it most. Then, just when I think I'm about to bury myself balls-deep, she stops.

Her green eyes stare down at me. "Put your hands up—on the headboard. If you let go, I stop."

I chuckle, but the look on her face tells me she's not joking.

So, obeying her command, I put my hands on the headboard, my fingers gripping it tightly. Without wasting any more time, she lowers onto me in one smooth motion. And it's fucking amazing.

She starts slowly—her pace ensuring I can feel every subtle move she makes. She puts her hands on my chest, using it for leverage as she starts to move faster.

"Fuck, T," I grit my teeth. My hands itch to grab her hips— to feel that thick ass underneath my fingertips.

But true to her word, the second my hands leave the headboard, Tracy stops.

"Put your hands back," she says, and when I don't do it right away, she rises up further on her knees, allowing me to slip out of her.

A groan of disappointment escapes my lips. I'm aware

that I could probably take control of this whole situation right now, but she's having way too much fun. Besides, it's nice seeing her entirely in her element.

Her hand reaches between her legs, rubbing as her eyes slightly roll back in her head. When her hand comes back into view, I can see her juices glistening on her fingers. She takes one of them and puts it to my lips. I suck on it, loving the sweet and tangy taste.

I need more.

So, I give in and do as she asks, putting my hands back on the headboard. This time, she wastes no time with teasing. Instead, she rides me like her life depends on it. She alternates between bouncing up and down and grinding against me.

Watching and not touching is killing me, but it feels too damn good to do anything to make her stop.

I watch her bring herself to orgasm, and I watch her rub her clit, wishing it was me doing it instead. Every time I come close to exploding inside her, though, she slows down, prolonging the experience.

The smirk on her face tells her she's loving being a little tease, but after about the fifth time of not being able to come, my patience is wearing thin.

My hands leave the headboard, but before she can process what's happening, I take charge and flip her over once more. This time, she's on her stomach beneath me.

Pulling her ass up in the air, I slide in from behind. She moans out as I get impossibly deep inside her. Then, once she's acclimated to my size, I slam into her hard and fast. She reaches down to rub her clit, and as I feel her tighten with another orgasm, finally exploding together.

We both collapse on the bed, our chests heaving.

"Sorry," I say. "I couldn't take the teasing anymore."

She smiles. "If you're going to fuck me like that, you never have to apologize."

Her hands wrap around my neck as she pulls me in for a kiss. We are both exhausted, yet her kiss is saying she's ready to go again. I swear I'm the luckiest man alive, and Tracy will never let me forget it.

"Ready for round two, wild child?" She asks, her fingers wrapping around my dick. It's beginning to grow hard again in her grip.

"Are you?"

She scoffs. "I could go all night."

"Baby girl, be careful what you wish for."

# Chapter Thirty-seven

## TRACY

Sunday, I sit in the middle of the store, going through all of the shelves and boxes, counting everything for inventory. I'm trying to get it done so that we can do dinner at Jessie's mom's this evening.

I haven't been to a family dinner at the Mitchell household in years, so I'm excited. I always loved going to eat over there. Annie has always been a fantastic cook, and I loved how busy and chaotic it all was. For a girl who was used to family dinners just consisting of her and her dad, eating with a big family was always entertaining. Now, I imagine it's even more so since the family has grown since then.

I've been here since about five AM, and I'm making pretty good time. Usually, Jamie comes in to help, but she had a wedding to go to today, so I told her I'd handle it. And it's easier just to do it myself than try to wrangle all the high-schoolers to focus long enough to teach them how to do it right.

Around lunchtime, there's a slight knock on the door. I sigh because apparently, someone can't read the sign saying we are closed to handle inventory.

But when I come around the corner, I can see that it's Jessie standing at the door with a bag of food in his hand.

Quickly, I unlock the door and let him in. "Hey, baby girl, I figured you were probably starving to death by now."

Warmth runs over me at his thoughtfulness. And as if right on cue, my belly makes a loud grumble.

We both laugh, and I lead him back to my office, and my nose tells me he brought tacos.

"Did you drive all the way out of town to get me those good tacos?" I ask. "You didn't have to do that."

"Oh, I think you're worth it. And I mean, I wanted tacos too." He winks, and one side of his mouth curls into a smile, showing off one of his cute dimples.

He pulls some food out of the bag, and we dig in.

"So, how's the inventory going?" He asks.

"Pretty good. I should be finished by this evening." I take a bite and remember just how wonderful these taste. "What have you been up to today?"

"I went home and did some cleaning and went and got a haircut." He pulls off his hat so that I can see.

I giggle. "It looks almost exactly the same."

He shrugs. "I like it like this."

"That's fair. It's not like I do much with my hair either."

Reaching out, he twists a lock of it around his finger. "I think it looks good."

When we finish eating, I expect him to head toward the door, but he rolls up his sleeves instead.

"What are you doing?" I ask.

"I'm here to help. I know you said you've got this all under control, but I figure two people are better than one. So, tell me what you need."

"You want to help me? In my women's clothing store?" I'm a little taken back because no man I've ever been around has taken an interest in my business or anything that goes along with it, except for my daddy. And even then, he just asks about it and pretends to be interested.

"Listen here, T," he begins. "This business is important to you, meaning that it's important to me. This is your dream, and I will do whatever I can to support that." He picks up a hot pink tank top. "That includes being a male model if you need me to.

You just say the word."

I giggle and try to keep the drink of soda I just took from coming out of my nose. "I would love to see that."

"Say no more." Without hesitation, he pulls his white t-shirt over his head and replaces it with the tank top. It stretches over his large frame, pulling the fabric to its breaking point.

"You're going to rip that," I say.

He stands up and walks over to the mirror, sashaying his hips along the way. When he gets there, his hand rests on his hip.

"You're just jealous of how good I look right now." He reaches up to touch his nipples which are hard and poking through the thin fabric. "I think I need bigger boobs to fill it out, though."

"You and me both," I mutter.

He walks back over to me and sits down. "You better not be talking shit about your boobs. I happen to love those boobs."

Looking down, I say, "They're not very big. Half the time, I don't even need a bra."

"And you think that's a bad thing? Easier access, baby girl." He grins a wicked smile that tells me he's thinking about my boobs.

I lean in closer to his face—almost close enough to kiss those sexy lips of his. But I don't. Instead, I whisper, "It's hard to take you seriously while you're wearing that shirt."

He stands back up. "Get used to it, buttercup. I'm buying it. Now, let's get to work."

I wonder if he's kidding, but the way he starts moving some boxes around tells me he is completely serious. Oh well, the crop top gives me a perfect view of his sexy stomach.

We spend the next couple of hours finishing up inventory. Jessie is a huge help and is terrific at helping get stuff done. It's mid-afternoon when we finish, so we still have some time before we have to be at dinner.

He walks over to me, setting his hands on the small of my back and pulling me close. "You're amazing. Do you know that?"

"How's that?"

"This." He gestures all around the store. "You did this. All of it. You took this store and made it your own, and you kick ass at everything you do."

"You're sweet." I smile and lean up to give him a soft kiss. "Now, are you going to take off the shirt?"

"I'll make you a deal. I'll take off the shirt if you try on a few things for me."

"You want me to try on clothes?"

He shrugs. "Just a couple."

I'm not sure what he's up to, but I'll play along. "Okay, fine. Pick me out a couple of things to try on."

His grin is infectious, and he wastes no time walking around the store picking out a few different things. When he returns, he has a flannel shirt, some jean shorts, and a dress.

"That's it?" I ask.

"For now."

Grabbing the top and shorts, I walk back toward my office.

Jessie calls after me, "I don't get to watch you change?"

"There are windows!"

Quickly, I step out of my own clothes and slide on the new ones. When I walk back out to show him, I'm surprised to find him over in my usual photo staging area. When Nicole comes in to model the new clothes, I have her pose in front of a backdrop in the store's back corner.

Jessie is now sitting back there, holding the large camera.

"What are you doing?" I ask.

"Just humor me, okay?"

Rolling my eyes, I step in front of the white backdrop and cross my arms in front of my chest.

"Come on, baby girl. I know you can do better than that. Pose for me." He holds the camera up and stares through the lens.

I set my hands on my hips and give a slight smile. The flash goes off as he snaps a quick photo.

"Next pose," he calls.

This time, I use the stool that's sitting there as a prop first to sit on and then lean over.

"Gorgeous! Gorgeous!" He calls in a terrible British accent.

When I can't help but smile, he snaps a string of pictures in a row. "There we go! That's the smile I've been waiting for."

Once he has taken at least 25 photos, he tells me to change into the dress.

*Okay, bossy.*

As I change into the dress, I decide to make things a little more interesting. I lift the dress enough to pull my panties down my legs. When they drop to the floor, I toss them onto the pile of my other clothes.

*Okay, I'm going to have to buy this dress. I'm not going to try to sell it after I go commando.*

I make my way back to where Jessie stands, scrolling through the photos on the camera.

"You ready?" I ask.

"Ready when you are." The smile he gives me makes me damn near weak in the knees.

I start with the typical poses as the flash goes off with every click of the camera. As we get further into it, I get a bit more daring and move to sit on the stool. My fingers slowly raise the hem of the sundress further and further. When it's just far enough, I let my thighs fall open, exposing my bare pussy.

Jessie brings the camera down from his eye and looks at me. "Baby girl, did you forget your panties?"

I shrug. "Didn't forget. Just decided to take them off."

He shakes his head back and forth, and in one swift motion, he sets the camera down and moves toward me. His mouth is on mine before I can even breathe.

His arms wrap around me and pull me so my body presses against his. His hands roam all over me before eventually making their way under the dress and grabbing a handful of my ass.

He growls into our kiss before pulling back to look at me. "Your office. Now."

"You don't want to do it right here?" I look around.

"You said it yourself—windows."

I turn around to head in that direction and feel a light swat on my ass. "Faster."

Once we are in the office, he shuts the door behind us—just in case. I'm standing in front of my desk as he walks up behind me. One of his hands wraps around my neck, holding me in place, while the other reaches between my legs. His finger finds my clit and starts to rub slow circles, and I can barely sit still.

His teeth nip the flesh on the back of my neck, making goosebumps cover every inch of my skin.

The hand around my neck slips under the straps of the dress and starts pinching my nipple. All of the sensations are making my legs feel like jelly. Heat begins to spread through my lower half.

Before I can go any further, though, he pulls both hands off my body. He brings the hand that was in between my legs up to his mouth and licks his finger.

I don't know what about that is so hot, but damn. My panties would catch fire—if I were wearing any.

He bends me over, so my chest is resting on the cool wood of my desk. I'm on a stack of papers, but I really don't care.

"I told you I was going to bend you over this desk, didn't I?" He asks, pulling up the dress, so my ass and pussy are exposed.

His hand gives a quick slap to my ass before pulling his cock out of his jeans and pushes inside my wetness.

My moan fills the room as I savor the feeling of him rubbing against my g-spot in just the right way. Between now and him fucking me from behind last night, I'm beginning to really love this position.

His fingers dig into my hips as my own fingers grasp the edge of the desk.

"You like teasing me, don't you, baby girl?" He asks.

It feels so good I can barely speak, so I just enthusiastically nod.

He fucks me hard and fast until I'm about to scream his name with my release, but then he slows down to an excruciatingly slow pace.

"Now, it's my turn to tease you, baby girl," he says in that deep Southern drawl.

In our time apart, the man has definitely found his naughty side and dirty mouth. And it might be my favorite thing in the entire world.

I push my ass back on him, encouraging him to give me all he's got.

"You don't play fair," he moans, watching me move back and forth on his cock. "Such a naughty girl."

It only takes a moment more of me moving on him before he grabs my hips and slams into me once again. This time though, there is no teasing. Instead, this time he keeps up his hard, fast tempo until my pussy is tightening around him as I come.

He groans as he empties into me before leaning down to string kisses along my shoulders.

"Woman, you are fucking incredible," he says, out of breath.

Still barely able to speak, I instead start laughing.

He looks at me. "It's not nice to laugh while my penis is still out."

"No, I was just thinking about how I *definitely* have to buy this dress now."

"I'll buy it for you...on one condition."

"What's that?" I ask.

"You aren't allowed to ever wear panties underneath it."

# Chapter Thirty-eight

## JESSIE

After we get done at the store, we head home to take showers and get ready to have dinner with my family. My momma asked that we show up a little early so I can finally talk to Jenna. It might be easier before everyone else gets there.

"What are you going to say to her?" Tracy asks me on the drive over.

"I'm not sure. I don't really remember how to speak *teenage girl*. Do you just want to talk to her for me?"

She shakes her head. "Nope. She's mad at *you.* I like your sister, and I don't want her to turn her attitude toward me."

"Well, do you have any advice?"

She thinks for a moment before looking at me. "Listen to her. Actually listen to what she has to say. Most people just write off teenage girls for being too emotional and crazy—and they sometimes are. But that doesn't mean that what they're feeling isn't real. It's *very* real to them. So just listen to her and try to see her side."

I can't help but smile. Tracy will make a great mom someday. I'm not going to tell her that because it will completely freak her out, but if she ever decides to have kids, she will be damn good at it.

Five minutes later, we pull up to my momma's house. I

park in the grass so that no one blocks us in if we decide to leave early.

I open up Tracy's door for her, and we head inside. She opted for a black sweater along with some dark blue jeans and her cowgirl boots. She looks beautiful.

Then again, I think she always looks beautiful, so maybe I'm slightly biased.

Once we are inside, we immediately head toward the kitchen. Momma stops cooking long enough to come over and give us both hugs.

"Tracy!" She exclaims. "I'm so glad my son got his head out of his ass and realized he was lost without you."

"Thanks, Momma," I mumble.

She laughs. "You know I'm just kidding—kind of."

This time, we all chuckle before she walks back over to the stove.

Tracy nudges me, and when I don't say anything, she asks, "So, where's Jenna?"

Momma sighs. "Oh, where else? Upstairs in her bedroom. I swear that girl spends so much time up there I'm convinced she's practicing witchcraft or something."

"Yeah, Momma. That's clearly the most logical thing that she's up there doing," I mutter.

Tracy practically pushes me out of the kitchen and toward the stairs. "Go," she commands, pointing upward.

As I trudge up the stairs, I consider going into one of the other bedrooms and just pretending that this conversation happened. But Tracy can tell when I'm full of shit, and it would never work.

When I reach Jenna's door, there is a giant **GO AWAY** sign on it along with some yellow police tape.

"Charming," I whisper to myself.

My knuckles lightly knock, but I get no answer. So, I knock again, this time louder.

When she still doesn't answer, I slowly open the door. The room is empty, but the window is open. As I walk closer, I see that she is sitting outside on the awning.

*What the hell is she doing out there?*

But when I see her take a drag off of her cigarette, I answer my own question.

Poking my head out the window, I make eye contact with her.

She sighs, "Shit."

"What's up, sis?" I ask, crawling out the window to sit next to her.

"Are you going to give me some huge lecture?" She asks.

"Jenna, I don't think I'm a person who is in any position to be giving you a lecture. I've done too many dumb things to have that right."

She puts out the cigarette on the shingles and then fiddles with the butt. "Then, why are you here?"

"Well, it's no secret that you've been mad at me for a while now. So, I figure it's about time you and I talk about it."

"Pass." She goes to stand up, but I grab her arm.

"How about you talk to me, or I go inside and tell Momma about what you've been doing out here? You know she will nail your window shut in a heartbeat."

Defeated, she sits back down. "Talk."

"You go first. You need to tell me why you're so mad."

"It's not my job to tell you!" She snaps.

"You're right. But I'm a guy, so I need a little bit of help. I'll tell you something, Jenna...men are dumb. We don't do subtlety well, and we sure as hell aren't mind readers. You have to break it down for us on the most basic level."

She's quiet for a moment before she says, "You left."

"Jen, I know I shouldn't have gone to Nashville. It was a mistake. Trust me—a *big* mistake. But I was 18 and just ready to get out of here."

Her head snaps toward me. "Jessie, I'm not mad at you for going to Nashville. Lord knows I plan to get out of here when I turn 18. I'm mad at you for not coming back."

"What do you mean? I'm back now?"

"And where were you when Daddy came back? When he came back here to die? Where were you when Momma had to take in the man who hurt her for so many years? You left everyone here to clean up the mess. Even at the funeral, you showed up for the service and ran back to Nashville."

"At least Jared and Jonas were around sometimes, but here —in this house—it was just Momma and me. Do you know how hard it is to help take care of a man who has been terrible to everyone you love? And after he was gone, did you check in—on Momma *or* me?"

Guilt hits me like a punch in the gut. I always had so many issues with my dad that I never stopped to think about Jenna's issues with him. When Daddy was around, he tried to act like I was his Golden Boy, but with Jenna, he barely acted like she existed. You'd think that she would have been daddy's little girl. She wasn't. Hell, Jenna was born right around the time that he started having issues with drugs and alcohol. She never even got to see the good man who the addict replaced.

"Shit, Jenna," I mutter. "I never even thought about it like that."

"Clearly." She rolls her eyes.

"Hey, can you cut the sarcasm for just a minute so that I can apologize to you?"

She simply looks at me. This time, her eyes a little softer.

"I really am sorry, Jenna. I had my own issues with that man, and honestly, I was worried that I might have killed him with my bare hands if I showed up back here. And I think part of me was mad at Momma for taking him in. She should have let him die on the street since that's where he liked to be so much." My tone is angry and filled with malice.

"I felt that way too," she begins. "But you know Momma. She would never do that. She's much too good for that—she's better than any of us will ever be."

"Then, why do you give her such a hard time?" I ask. "Rumor has it you've been a pretty big pain in the ass lately."

In typical teenage fashion, she rolls her eyes again. "Because she drives me insane. She tries to pry into every aspect of my life and questions everything I do."

"Isn't that what mothers are supposed to do?"

She simply shrugs her shoulders.

"Jenna, you have to think about it from her point of view. I sort of went off the rails, and she doesn't want that to happen with you. She let me go out into the big, bad world, and it swallowed me up and spat me out. Plus, that woman raised three boys but always wanted a little girl. Have you ever thought that maybe she's just trying to bond with you? Maybe she's just trying to have that whole 'mother-daughter relationship' thing."

"Maybe," she says in barely more than a whisper.

"Just cut the woman some slack. And for what it's worth, I really am sorry."

She looks at me and nods, tucking a strand of her long, blonde, curly hair behind her ear. "It's alright."

"No, it's not, but I promise to do my best to make it better going forward."

And lo and behold, my sister actually smiles at me. That may be the first smile I've seen from her since I got back.

She asks. "So, are you going to tell Momma about me smoking out here?"

I shake my head and say, "Nah, it'll be our secret. But I'll give you some advice that someone just recently gave me. No one is going to want to kiss you when you smell like an ashtray."

I about fall off the roof when she replies, "Oh, trust me. I don't have to worry about that. All the boys I kiss smoke too."

My hands fly over my ears. "Whoa, Jenna! Way too much information!"

When I put my hands down, she's just giggling. Her head leans over and rests on my shoulder. If I didn't know any better, I'd think she missed me. But I won't say that to her because she's likely to not talk to me for months on end again.

Instead, my sister and I look out over the yard in silence, and I let the memories of this place wash over me.

# *Chapter thirty-nine*

### JESSIE

*E* *leven years ago...*

"Jessie, where are you going?" My father asks. He sips his coffee without looking up from his newspaper.

"Out," I scoff, still heading toward the door.

"That's not an answer." Still no eye contact.

My momma walks into view, setting a plate of eggs in front of him. "Jessie, where are you going?"

I really don't want to give him the satisfaction of an answer, but I make it a point never to be rude to my momma. "Tracy and I are going to ride our bikes for a while."

That gets the old bastard to put his paper down. "You spend too much time with that girl."

"Funny, I don't think we spend nearly enough time together," I respond with all the annoyance I can muster.

"When did you become such a smartass?"

"I guess it was while you were *away*." I use air quotes to assure him that all of us know about his bad habits.

This is the first time he's been home in eight months. I think that's the longest stint ever. I never know exactly where he is, and I'm fairly positive I don't want to know. I guarantee it's not good, though.

Jenna and I think maybe he has a whole other life—maybe complete with a whole other family. Neither one of us will ever say that to our momma, though.

I'm still confused as to why she lets the no-good-son-of-a-bitch keep coming back. She's probably doing it for us—like we are desperate to have our father around.

But honestly, I think all of us would rather he stay gone.

Well, Jonas and Jared probably don't care as much because they've already moved out. However, Jenna and I are still here, and we want him gone.

Every time he comes home, he's got some magical story about how he got clean and how things will be different.

When I was younger, I'd believe him every time. After all, he's my dad, and I wanted to see the good in him. But all of his broken promises were enough to ensure I would never believe him again.

I can just barely remember when he was halfway normal. He still wasn't father of the year, but he was at least present. And funny. The man actually used to be funny. Granted, they were always lame Dad jokes, but when I was little, they were hysterical.

After he first got hurt, he was home from work for a while. At first, he was in too much pain to do much of anything, but when he started on the painkillers, things changed. For a while, he was always taking me out. We would go fishing and hunting. Jared and Jonas were old enough to be too cool to hang out with their dad, and Jenna was still a baby. So that left all of his attention focused on me.

To this day, I think Jared and Jonas still resent me for it. They think I got some sort of special treatment from him. I don't think it was that I was his favorite—more like a lack of options.

Whatever it was, though, it was pretty short-lived. It didn't take long for him to get addicted to the medicine and then turn his attention toward other vices.

I zone out as he starts griping at me about how I need to focus more on swimming and less on trying to get a piece of ass. When I broke out as the star of the school swim team, he started pushing me to practice all the time—acting like nothing else in life matters.

Yes, swimming is important. I'm working on getting a scholarship, but I know the only reason he pushes me is because he sees an eventual cash cow. That was made apparent when he talked to Momma about hiring a coach to get me into the Olympics.

I'm under no delusions that I am going to be some world champion. I just want to get a scholarship to get out of this town and go to college. After that, I couldn't care less about swimming.

As he's going on and on about my 'future', I take a good look at him. The drugs and alcohol have remarkably aged him. He and my momma are only a few weeks apart in age, but he looks years older. His hair, once dark and similar to mine, is now mostly grey. His eyes are sunken in, and he's got large dark circles underneath each one. And his hand shakes every time he picks up his mug, telling me he's probably going through some sort of withdrawal.

When I tune back into what he's talking about, I hear him saying how he thinks Tracy is a bad influence on me. My blood boils at him talking shit when he doesn't know a single thing about her.

I cut him off, "You don't get to talk about who's a bad influence on me. When you stop all of your bad habits, you can have a say-so about who is in my life. Until that moment, I don't want to hear it."

He turns to my momma with hopes she will defend him, but she doesn't.

She just looks at me and says, "Go on, get out of here. Tell Tracy I say hi."

Before I hit the door, I hear my father call, "I thought we could spend some time together tonight."

That makes me stop in my tracks. Then, turning around, I say, "Since you're going to be here permanently, I guess we can do that whenever."

A look passes between us—a look that says we both know that he won't be around permanently.

I give it a week—tops.

# Chapter Forty

## TRACY

"Can I help with anything?" I ask Annie as she moves around the kitchen with ease. The woman makes cooking a meal for eight people look effortless.

"No, sweetie, I'm good. You just sit there and relax. Jessie told me that you had a rough day at work."

I struggle not to chuckle at how the word 'rough' could be used to describe our sexy romp on my desk.

I look around the warm and inviting kitchen. It hasn't changed much over the years aside from a few upgrades to the appliances. I remember spending many evenings over here eating dinner. Often, my daddy was working late, and Annie didn't want me to have to fend for myself. It wasn't like she was looking down on him for having to work—more so just wanting to help out however she could.

After my momma died, Annie always made sure I knew that I had another safe place to go. She never minded when I was over. I don't know that I can ever thank her enough for that.

"So, how are you and Jessie doing?" She asks, pulling me out of my thoughts.

"We are good," I respond.

"He still doing alright?"

It feels like she's fishing for information, and I don't really want to talk about him behind his back. He gets enough of that from everyone else.

She must notice my apprehension because she adds, "Oh, listen to me, sounding like a nosey ol' fool. I was just asking because I know since coming back to Grady, the transition has been hard on him."

When I look at her, I don't see a nosey ol' fool, though. All I see is a mother worried about her son.

"He's good," I say. "Really good."

Her warm smile lights up the room. "I'm glad to hear that. I've always said that you were good for that boy."

I feel my cheeks warm a bit listening to someone else acknowledge how good our relationship is—how right it all feels. I'm about to tell her how much I appreciate it, but the front door swings open, and the sound of shoes running across the floor fills the air. Seconds later, Jonas, Andi, and their two boys appear.

"My babies!" Annie yells, giving the boys each a kiss on the top of their heads while wrapping them in hugs.

"Hey, Momma," Jonas greets before giving her a peck on the cheek. Then, he looks over at me. "Hi, Tracy. How's it going?"

"Good, thanks," I answer.

Greetings are barely exchanged when the door opens again, and Jared and his daughter, Macey, come in. Annie loves on Macey just like she did Keith and Kyle, and Jared kisses Annie just like Jonas did.

I can tell that this is just their regular Sunday routine. They all come together once a week to just be with each other. I can't say I'm not a little envious. Of course, if Jessie and I last, I guess this will be my typical Sunday evening too.

Not wanting to jump the gun, though, I try to get those thoughts out of my head.

"Hey, Tracy," Jared smiles. "Where is that annoying little brother of mine?"

Before I can answer, Jessie walks into the room. "Right here, asshole."

"*You're* an asshole!" Jared snaps back.

"Language!" Annie shouts.

"Sorry, Momma," they both groan in unison.

"Dinner is in ten minutes!" She announces.

The kids run out back to play for a few minutes, leaving all the adults making small talk in the kitchen. It's loud, crazy, and chaotic.

I love it.

I don't speak much, instead listening to all the conversations going on around me. Finally, Jessie comes over, taking a seat next to me. He runs his hand up and down my thigh as he talks to his brothers and mom.

Andi keeps trying to talk to me, but every time she tries, either Jonas asks her something, or one of the boys runs in to tell her something.

Once dinner is made, the kids come back inside to wash up, and all of us move into the dining room and have a seat at the larger table. After everyone is settled, large dishes of meatloaf, mashed potatoes, corn, green beans, and homemade bread are all passed around so everyone can fill their plates.

And it's delicious—as usual. Anything Annie Mitchell makes is fantastic.

I eat my weight in the excellent food. Here, with all these Mitchell boys, no one bats an eye when I go in for seconds.

After everyone finishes, Jessie stands up to clear the table. When I follow him to help, he insists that I sit back down, but I hate feeling useless. So, I continue to clear off the table and start washing some of the dishes.

"You don't have to do that, you know?" Jessie asks.

"I'm your guest. It's the least I can do."

He turns me to face him, resting his hands on my hips. "That's where you're wrong, baby girl. You're not a guest. You're family—you're part of *this* family, and I'm sorry I didn't see that before, but I will damn sure remind you of it from here on out."

"You're a real smooth-talker, wild child," I say, leaning my head against his chest.

"Smooth enough to get you out of your panties?" He jokes.

"Sweets, you know you barely have to talk at all to make

that happen."

He laughs and pulls me in closer for a hug. His arms wrapped around me feels so right.

"Well, aren't you two just cutest?" Annie asks, walking back into the room.

"As a matter of fact, we are," Jessie says. "But it's been a long day, Momma. So, I think we are going to head home. We both have work tomorrow, so it'll be an early morning."

"Okay, dear. You guys get out of here. Thanks for gracing us with your presence." She winks at him before giving us both hugs. When she hugs me, she whispers, "I'm always here. If you need anything, just let me know."

I thank her, and we head out. I scoot close to Jessie in the truck and get settled in the crook of his arm. It's a short drive home, and we just quietly listen to the soft hum of the song on the radio.

Once we get back to my place and head inside, I busy myself with doing up the few dishes in the sink.

"Are you just going to do dishes everywhere we go today?" Jessie asks.

I chuckle. "Eh, there's not that many of them. I might as well get them done."

"How about you leave them for tomorrow?" He asks, kissing the back of my neck.

"You're awfully distracting." Goosebumps break out all over the tender flesh.

"You haven't seen anything yet," he says, his hands moving upward and grazing over the fabric of my shirt.

I lean back into him, letting my ass graze against his groin. I can feel him getting hard through his jeans.

"You are so bad," he whispers in my ear.

"Speak for yourself," I moan as his fingers pinch my nipples.

My head falls against him as one arm reaches back, wrapping around his neck—my other grabbing the bulge in his jeans.

His fingers move from my breast down to my shorts, undoing the button and tugging them down my legs, taking my underwear with them. He leans down to help me step out of them and gently bites the soft flesh of my ass.

Once the bottom half of me is naked, he walks me over to the table and lays me down on it. As he unzips his own pants, I spread my legs for him, giving him a perfect view of what's waiting for him.

It doesn't take long at all before I feel him sliding into me. He stands on the side of the table, holding onto my legs as he gives me everything he has. The way he is ramming me hard and fast tells me that this will not last long.

So, I guess it's a good thing that he is hitting all the right spots and begins rubbing my clit to speed along my orgasm.

Neither one of us are entirely naked, and it's in no way 'romantic,' but holy hell, is it hot. There is something so sexy about the fact that we just had to have each other right then and there.

This man makes me lose all control. He satisfies the wild side that I've tried so hard to tame down over the years—gets the storm brewing without ever letting me turn into a full-blown hurricane.

He thrusts into me faster and faster until we both cry out the others name while we find our releases.

When we finish, he takes my hand and leads me into the shower. We step inside and let the hot water wash over us. Jessie holds me close, wrapping his arms around me. Our naked bodies touch, but there's nothing sexual about it.

He pulls my chin up to look at him. "Hey, earlier when I told you that you're family, I meant it. I want you to be part of my family, and I want you and me to be a family of our own. I've said it before, but I want you to really hear me when I say it. I am in this. I'm all in. I want this thing—you and me—to be a forever kind of thing."

Tears sting behind my eyes because I've really never cared much about relationships or about love, but now that it's here, I'm deliriously happy. In this moment, I'm happier than I've ever been.

And I pray to God that we get to stay right here...in this moment.

# Chapter Forty-one

## TRACY

The next couple of weeks seem to pass in a blur. Jessie and I are trying our hands at domestic life, and so far, it seems to be going great. Our days are filled with work, and our evenings are filled with loving each other. Well, most nights. Some nights, we are just too exhausted and fall asleep before we get to the fun stuff.

Those nights seem special, too, though. It's nice just to feel him next to me. Lately, we both seem more tired than usual. It's not surprising with Jessie working at the ranch. I don't know what my excuse is.

Most times, we stay at my place, but occasionally, we go to his. We even had dinner with Andi, Jonas, and the boys one night. There is just a certain ease to it all, which I certainly appreciate.

On one of my days off that Jessie is working, I decide to have lunch with Andi. Instead of going out, she is ordering in, so I head over to her house. The boys are both in school for the day, and our men are both working, so we plan to have some much-needed girl time.

When I arrive, she gives me a big hug and basically yanks my arm out of the socket, pulling me inside.

"Whoa! What's the rush?" I ask. She continues to lead me through the house until we get to the back door.

"I thought we could hang out on the deck," she says. "And what's the hurry? I live with three boys. I am around testosterone 24/7, and I am in desperate need of some female interaction."

"Driving you crazy?"

"In a manner of speaking." She smiles. "Don't get me wrong. I love my boys, but no one ever told me how many sound effects they make. When they play, everything that comes out of their mouth is a sound effect. It's been a while since I was a kid, but I don't remember doing that."

"Me either. It's probably just a boy thing."

"And the dirt. Oh boy, the dirt. I don't bother spending too much money on clothes because they get them dirty twenty minutes after putting them on. It's like they have a radar that leads them to every single mud puddle on this ranch—not to mention they grow out of everything in what seems like a week after I buy it."

I just laugh listening to her vent.

She pauses for a moment and looks at me. "Listen to me. I sound so ungrateful. The truth is that I've never been happier."

I stop her before she can go any further. "I know that, but *the truth is* that it's okay to complain sometimes. I'm sure all of this has been completely new for you."

She lets out a loud sigh. "It has been, but I wouldn't trade it for anything. And as far as dads go, Jonas is right up there with the best of them. A lot of men wouldn't have wanted to take on two kids that weren't their own—especially two kids who have already had a hard life so far."

"Well, there is a bright side to that," I say with a smile.

"Yeah? What's that?"

"You guys got to skip the diaper stage."

We both laugh before she walks inside to grab us some snacks. When she reappears, she holds a large tray with assorted meats, cheeses, and crackers.

"Don't worry," she says, setting the tray down on the table between us. "All I did was open packages and spread them out on the tray, so they're safe to eat."

"Good. Wouldn't want you cooking anything."

"Haha," she replies sarcastically. "You want something to drink? Maybe some wine?"

"Just water," I answer. "My stomach has been a little upset, so I'm trying not to make it worse with booze."

"Fair enough." She disappears into the house for a few moments before bringing me out a water and herself a glass of wine.

When she sits back down, she asks how things are going with Jessie and I.

I grab a cracker to munch on and a drink of water before answering. "Good. Really good actually. I know so many people in this town think of Jessie as just a screw-up or a druggie, but really, he's not like that."

"I know," she interrupts. Of course, she would know. Jessie is her brother-in-law.

"And I mean we have both lived our lives the past seven years, but when we are together, it's like we sort of picked up where we left off—except it's better now. We aren't just a couple of dumb kids who don't know what they want out of life. I think we can really make a go out of this thing. Hell, we've been spending almost every free moment together for a while now. In fact, I think tonight will be the first night we haven't spent together in weeks."

"Why not tonight?"

"He's not feeling well."

She leans back. "Stomach issues like you?"

I shake my head. "No, I'm pretty sure it's just a bad cold. He's got a stuffy nose, cough, and sore throat. He decided to stay at his place tonight, so I won't get feeling any worse. But, honestly, I think I'd rather get sick and still have him with me."

"Look at you." She smiles. "You look so cute—all swoony and in love."

My mouth hangs open. "You're crazy. I do not swoon."

"That's not what it looks like from where I'm sitting."

"Then, move your seat," I tease.

She laughs. "Okay, okay. I get it. You don't want to be told how cute you guys are. It's just nice to see you happy."

"Thanks," I reply with a slight smile.

I change the subject back to her, and she talks more about Jonas and the kids. I don't mind listening. As happy as she is, I can understand still needing a sounding board every once in a while.

We talk for a bit before she asks, "So, do you want me to tell me what's up with you?"

"What do you mean?"

"I mean, since you've been sitting out here, you've barely eaten anything. And what you have eaten has been nothing but crackers."

"What's wrong with that?" I scoff.

"Well, I bought extra of everything because I thought I would for sure have to refill the tray. I'm pretty sure you eat more than Jonas does. *And* you've been drinking water."

"I like water!" I defend.

"Not during a girls' day."

"I told you my stomach has just been upset. I've just been watching what I eat to not make it worse. It's probably a stomach bug or something."

"Damn, that sucks. How long has it been going on for?"

My shoulders shrug. "I don't know. Maybe a week and a half."

"You think you have a stomach bug that has lasted a week and a half?"

"I mean, I guess. I don't have a fever or anything, so I don't imagine it's anything worse than that."

"Depends on how you define *worse*," she says almost under her breath.

"What are you talking about?"

"Well, you have felt sick to your stomach, aren't eating much, and have felt super tired lately, right?" She asks.

"Yeah. So?"

She sets her wine glass down on the table and leans in close. "Trace, have you considered the possibility that you might be pregnant?"

*******************************************************

When Andi suggested I was pregnant, I told her she was fucking nuts. But here I am, staring down at a little stick that shows two bright blue lines.

There is no 'maybe' here. It is clear as fucking day.

"How did this happen?" I ask Andi as she sits in my bathroom with me.

When she brought up her little theory, I was entirely freaked out and had to take a test just to calm myself down. Not wanting to be seen in the middle of Grady buying a pregnancy test, we drove two towns over to pick one up.

She rolls her eyes. "I think we know *how* this happened."

I playfully smack her in the arm. "You know what I mean. I have been on the pill since I was 18. Shouldn't that have built up some sort of wall shielding all sperm from entering my uterus?"

She laughs. "I don't think it works that way. Besides, they say after a while, your body can build up a tolerance to it, so it might not be as effective."

I stand up so fast that I knock everything off the bathroom sink. "What?! Why wouldn't someone tell me that? Why wouldn't that be listed on the packaging?"

She shrugs. "I don't know if it's actually true or not. Just sort of an old wives' tale."

"Those old wives can go to hell," I spit.

"Do you want to talk about it?"

I close the toilet seat and slump back down on it. "What is there to talk about? I'm going to have a baby."

"Well, how do you feel about that?"

Tears sting behind my eyes, but I try my hardest to keep them at bay. "I don't know, Andi. I've never really thought much about it. It's always been a possibility that I could be a mom, but you know me—I live life in the moment and try not to think too far ahead. I certainly didn't think kids were in my future anytime soon."

"I get it, but that's not necessarily a bad thing. A baby is life-changing, but it doesn't mean that one is life-ruining."

"I know that. I just…I don't know. Jessie and I are in such a good place. And things are so good with the business, and now, I'm going to have to give it up."

She stops me. "Why do you assume that you have to give up your business?"

"Come on, Andi, we've already had this talk. The writing is on the wall. I can't have it all."

"I think you're wrong."

I could sit here and argue with her all day, but I don't want to. I just don't have the strength. Besides, I don't think I should be talking anymore about this to anyone until I talk to Jessie. Not to mention, I could use a little bit of time to myself.

I tell Andi that I'm exhausted and think I should lie down for a bit. She is reluctant to leave me alone but does it anyway—after a hug that seems to last forever.

Once she's gone, I go lie on the bed. My stomach feels queasy, but I don't know if it's the baby or the sudden sense of dread that I'm feeling.

I'm unsure of absolutely everything right now except one thing:

I need to talk to Jessie.

Pulling out my phone, I type out a simple text.

**Hey, I know you're still feeling crappy, but I need to see you tonight.**

# Chapter Forty-two

## JESSIE

I pull my phone out of my pocket and look at the text I just got from Tracy. She wants to meet up tonight. We had agreed not to get together since I'm sick, but if she wants to see me, I'm not going to tell her no. My fingers type her back a reply.

**Sounds good, baby girl.**

Although we don't go over any details, I figure I will go home and shower after I get off and then head over to her house.

I sniffle loudly and shove my phone back in my pocket before getting back to work. I'm moving some haybales outside to the different cattle pens, and I just can't wait for this day to be over. This job is exhausting enough without a head cold looming over me.

"Dude, you look like shit," Jonas says, walking up behind me.

"Yeah, well, I'm sick. What's your excuse?" I taunt.

"Oh, you're jealous of my good looks," he jokes, rubbing his chest.

I can't help but laugh at how ridiculous he looks, but when he says he has a favor to ask, I stop.

He sighs. "I have to get out of here. I guess Kyle fell off his bike and hurt his knee. He's probably going to need stitches, and it's Taylor's day off. Do you think you can finish up around here?

I know you're sick, and I normally wouldn't ask—"

I hold up my hand and cut him off. "It's fine, Joe. Go. I've got this."

"Thanks, Jess. I owe you one." He's gone in a flash.

I sit down on one of the hay bales and rest for a minute before getting back to work. I'm going to try to get it done as fast as possible to get to Tracy, but I imagine I'll be here a while.

My fingers find my pocket and trace the small circular object inside. I pull it out to look at it—probably my fifth time looking at it today alone.

What am I doing with an engagement ring? I mean, it's only been about a month since Tracy and I found our way back to each other.

But damnit, it's been the best month of my entire life.

I knew from the moment I kissed her again that I was one lucky son-of-a-bitch to have her back in my life, and I wasn't going to let her go. She means way too much to me.

I've always wanted to marry Tracy. Even when we were apart, I sought out girls who I thought mimicked her. But that didn't work. It turns out there is only one Tracy Kennedy.

I want to ask her to marry me, but I've hesitated—not because I have doubts. I don't. But I worry the speed of things will freak out Tracy.

I haven't planned some sort of epic proposal. I figure that when the time is right, I will know it. The perfect moment will eventually present itself.

Until then, I will carry this ring with me everywhere I go. And I hope to God that she will say yes to me when I ask.

If she does, I vow always to do my best to make her happy. She deserves nothing but the best, and I know that I may not always fit that bill, but I'll sure as shit try.

I stand up and try to shake off the light-headed feeling I just got. Unfortunately, cold meds and work aren't the best combination. My head is foggy, so I completely forget to text Tracy and make a plan. Instead, I get back to work, anxious to finish up everything that needs to be done so I can go see my woman.

# Chapter Forty-three

## TRACY

I have a pit in my stomach as I pull up outside Jessie's house. He told me he would have to work late and would stop by once he was done, but I just couldn't sit in my house any longer all alone.

Instead, I got in my car and drove over here, anxious to get this talk over with. I figure I'll just wait for him until he gets home. As I pull up in the driveway, I see a couple of lights on, so maybe he's already here and just in the shower.

I think about going in and joining him, but my mind is racing so fast that I don't know that I'd even be able to enjoy myself.

I step out of my Jeep and begin to head inside. The sound of music hits my ears before I even get to the door. I don't know what it is, but it certainly doesn't sound like the country music Jessie typically listens to.

Usually, I would just walk in, but something makes me pause. I'm not sure exactly what it is, but I decide to knock instead.

It takes a minute for the door to swing open, but when it does, it's not Jessie that is standing in front of me. Instead, it's some blonde woman who is wearing some very skimpy, very see-through lingerie.

*What in the literal fuck?*

The blonde smiles. "Hi, can I help you?"

I'm surprised I can get the words out when I say, "I'm looking for Jessie."

She gives me a smile that I am sure is meant to be warm, but all it makes me want to do is throw up. "Oh, he just ran next door for a minute. He should be back any time now. Do you want to come in and wait?"

My mind is moving so fast I can barely comprehend what's going on in front of me. This has to be some sort of horrible bad dream.

"I'm sorry, but who are you?" I ask. "Does Jessie know you?"

She giggles. "Well, I should hope so. We've been dating for a while now. I'm Gabby."

Gabby? As in the woman who is supposed to be his ex? The woman who had him so fucked up for years that he couldn't see straight? The woman he said he went to see in Nashville to tell her to leave him the fuck alone?

Either she didn't get the message...or he really didn't tell her that. The way things are looking right now, it appears to be the latter. I mean, how else would she know where he lives? How else would she get into his house? And why else would she be standing here in lingerie?

Has he been lying to me this whole time? I don't know when he would have had time to see her...unless it's like tonight when he told me he was working and apparently wasn't.

Has everything Jessie been saying to me been a lie?

Gabby pulls me from my thoughts. "And who are you?"

"Tracy," I mutter.

"Oh, right! He's told me so much about you two and your friendship!"

*Friendship? That's what he thinks this is?*

My blood starts to boil, and I'm at a loss for what to do.

Gabby says, "I'll be sure to tell him you stopped by."

"Don't bother," I grumble as I begin to walk away.

It isn't until I am safely back in the Jeep that I let my tears freely fall. I can't believe I was so fucking stupid. I fell for all of his sweet talk and his magic penis. How could I have been so blind? I'm pregnant with a cheater's baby.

I have no idea what to do, but I sure as shit don't want to hear any more of his lies once he hears I stopped by. I know he will try to call me, and I can't listen to any more of his bullshit.

But where the hell am I supposed to hide in Grady? Everywhere I go is going to be pretty damn easy for him to find me.

Guess it's time to go off the grid for a little while.

# Chapter Forty-four

## JESSIE

When my day is finally over, I walk as fast as my exhausted body will let me back to my place. Then, I plan to take a quick shower and head right over to Tracy's. After that, I'll pop some more cold meds in hopes that I feel somewhat normal this evening.

As I approach the house, though, something is off. I see lights on, and I hear music playing. After growing up with my extremely frugal mother, I never leave anything on when I leave for work.

Maybe Tracy is there waiting for me. That would make sense. After all, in a town like Grady, I never lock my doors.

Instead of walking around to the front, I enter through the back door. Once I'm inside, the choice of music immediately lets me know it's not Tracy. This pop-princess shit is the type of music to make Tracy nauseated.

My blood begins to boil as some blonde hair comes into sight.

Gabby.

She is wearing some very tiny lingerie which doesn't hide a single thing. What the fuck is she doing here?

I turn down the music and ask her just that.

When she hears me, she abruptly turns around. "Hey, baby!" She jogs over to me in the high heels she's wearing.

My arms reach out to touch her shoulders, stopping her before she gets to me.

"No, Gabby. No, 'hey baby.' Why the fuck are you here?"

"I came to see you. Thought I could stay here in Grady with you for a while."

Okay, this girl is seriously fucked up.

"Gabby, do you not remember our conversation? I told you I'm in love with someone else and have moved on. You told me you understood."

"Jessie, I know what you were really saying. You love this small town and were done with Nashville. So, I came here to be with you. We can be together anywhere—even in this small little map-dot town." She reaches out to touch me, but I back up, avoiding her hands.

"Gabby, you and I are done. We have been since I left Nashville. We have been done since I saw you sucking off your dealer. Do you even remember that?"

"I remember, and it was a mistake." She gives me a sultry smile and moves closer. "Aw, is someone jealous? How about I make it up to you? I'll suck your cock right now and remind you just how good it is."

Is she for real? No one can be this off their rocker.

"Gabby, I need you to listen to me. I don't want your mouth on me. In fact, I don't want any part of you near any part of me. How the fuck did you even find me?"

She shrugs. "You told me all about your life here in Grady when you came to Nashville. When I got into town, it wasn't hard to ask around to figure out where you were. You know—small town. People love to talk. And once I got here, I was just going to wait out front, but when the door was unlocked, I figured you must be here. I mean, your truck is out front."

Cutting her off, I spit, "I work on this ranch, Gabby. I don't need to drive my truck to work. Just because the door is unlocked doesn't mean you can just come in and make yourself at home."

Her face falls a little bit, and she pouts out her bottom lip. "I just wanted to be here waiting for you. I thought you'd be happy to see me. I even got all sexy for you."

My hand rubs against the stubble I have growing. "Gabby, this isn't happening. You shouldn't have come here. I'm in love with someone else."

Still not getting the message, she says, "I get that you have feelings for her, but I *know* you have feelings for me too. I don't care if you still care about her. Hell, invite her over; the three of us can have some fun."

Most men would relish the thought of that—two extremely sexy women in their bed at the same time. But for me, the idea of it makes me sick to my stomach. I am much more of a one-woman kind of man.

She just isn't getting how serious Tracy and I are. Pulling the ring out of my pocket, I hold it up.

"Gabby, look. This is the ring that I'm going to use to propose to Tracy. I want her to be my *wife.*"

She looks at the ring and then back at me as though something clicks. "You're going to marry her?"

I nod. "As long as she says yes."

"And if she doesn't say yes?" She asks.

"Then, I will keep trying until she does. I will spend every day trying to show her how much she means to me until she thinks I'm worthy of being her husband."

"Why her?" Her eyes gleam with tears.

"She's everything I've ever wanted. And Gabby, it's not that I didn't care about you. But I think I've been in love with Tracy ever since we were kids. That love has just evolved over the years."

She nods and walks over to throw on a pair of jeans and a t-shirt she has folded on my couch.

"I'm sorry, Gabby, but you should have never come here."

She gets her stuff together in silence. I have no idea if she is hearing what I'm saying, but if this doesn't work, I will have to take other action—although I have no idea what that action should be.

As she picks up her bag, she says, "I have a room booked

at the Grady Motel if you change your mind. I've already paid for the week, so I might stay there and try to compose myself before heading back to Nashville."

"Good luck, Gabby. But I won't change my mind."

I watch her blonde hair blow slightly as she opens the door. She takes one final glance back, and I hope and pray it's the last time I ever see Gabby.

Once she's gone, I think about what I'm going to tell Tracy, but I know there's only one option.

The truth.

I'm not going to hide something like this from her. Putting the ring away, I decide tonight is probably not the best time to pop the question. She's probably going to be mad as hell when I tell her about this.

I take a shower as quickly as I can, and when I step out, I hear pounding on my front door.

Angry pounding.

*What the hell is it now?*

I wrap a towel around my bottom half and jog to open it. When I swing it open, Andi is standing there. Her face is tight, and she looks pissed. I'm surprised smoke isn't coming out of her nostrils.

Slapping me in the chest, she asks, "What the fuck did you do?"

# Chapter Forty-five

## JESSIE

"Ouch!" I rub my chest where Andi just slapped me. "What was that for?"

She pushes past me, making her way into the living room. "What did you do to Tracy?"

"What do you mean? I haven't talked to Tracy since earlier. What are you talking about, Andi?" My heart thumps in my chest, hoping that nothing terrible happened to Tracy.

"I don't know, but she sent me this text." Pulling out her phone, she reads the word aloud. "Hey, just letting you know I'll be out of town for a few days. I don't know when I'll be back. Turning my phone off, so don't try to call. Caught Jessie cheating. I'll explain when I get home."

"What?!" I exclaim. "I didn't cheat on her!"

She keeps reading, "Went to his house, and his ex was there. Apparently, she's not his ex. I just…need to be alone for a few days. Talk soon."

Her piercing eyes look back at me, and everything starts to make a bit more sense.

"Son of a bitch," I mutter under my breath, taking a seat on the couch.

"Jessie, I swear you have five seconds to tell me what the hell is going on, or I swear I will kick your ass all the way back to Nashville."

"When I got home from work, Gabby was here."

"Gabby? The girl you dated in Nashville? The one who—"

I cut her off. "Yeah, her. A few weeks ago, she called me a lot, so I went to Nashville to tell her to leave me alone. It was over, and I was with Tracy. I thought that was the end of it, but I get here today, and she was here, half-naked and waiting for me."

"And you fucked her?" She looks appalled. "Especially when Tracy is—"

"No! I didn't fuck her!" I interrupt. "I told her that I was in love with Tracy and to get the hell out. I would never do that to T."

She leans back on the couch, crossing her arms. "Except back in high school, right?"

"Shit, Andi, that's a low blow. Back in high school, we both made mistakes. I have been trying ever since we got back together to make up for mine. And Tracy forgave me. I'm in love with her, and I just got her back. I'm not going to be an idiot and do anything to mess that up."

The look on her face shows she's still unsure of whether or not to believe me. I stand up and walk over to the small box where I keep that ultrasound photo. Now, it's also home to the engagement ring when it's not in my pocket.

I pull it out and turn back around. "I'm going to ask Tracy to marry me. Still think I'm just going to throw all that away?"

She stands up and walks over to me, taking the ring out of my hand. She examines it for a moment before handing it back to me. "Okay, I believe you. The next step is getting Tracy to believe you."

"Where do you think she'd go?" I ask.

She shrugs. "I don't know. You've known her much longer than I have. What do you think?"

I think for a moment. There's no way she'd go to our lake. She knows that is the first place that I'd look. Grady isn't a big town, and she knows that—not many places to hide.

"I have no idea," I finally say.

"Well, put on some clothes. Let's go try to find her."

\*\*\*\*\*\*\*\*\*\*\*\*\*\*\*\*\*\*\*\*\*\*\*\*\*\*\*\*\*\*\*\*\*\*\*\*\*\*\*\*\*\*\*\*\*\*\*\*\*\*\*\*\*\*\*\*\*\*\*\*\*\*\*\*

It's been over a day, and Andi and I have had no luck finding Tracy. She's not home. She told her manager at the shop that she was taking a few days off. Andi said she would talk to Tracy's dad, but I'm not holding my breath.

I've searched this whole town, and she seems to have disappeared entirely. I'm sure that's the way she wants it.

Everything is so fucked up. The woman I love is hiding from me because of a giant misunderstanding. But that's what I described the thing back in high school as too, isn't it? A misunderstanding?

How many misunderstandings am I going to ask her to overlook?

Damnit, I should have already asked her to marry me. Maybe with that ring on her finger, she wouldn't have fallen for Gabby's bullshit.

Maybe not.

I am a pretty big fuck-up. Maybe this is just the straw that broke the camel's back. Maybe she finally realized that she's way too good for me.

I shake my head as if trying to fling all of the negativity out of it.

No, fuck that. I'm in love with Tracy, and I know I can make her happy. I would give everything I have to make her the happiest woman in the world.

And when I see her again, I will get on my knees and beg if I have to. I love her so damn much.

Not knowing where else to go, I pull up in Tracy's driveway. I don't know where is she is. I don't know when she's coming back, and I don't know if she will even want to see me when she does.

But one thing I know for sure:

I'm going to sit right here in this driveway until she returns.

# Chapter Forty-six

## TRACY

As I sit in my lawn chair next to the fire I've made, I try to relax. Usually, camping is something that eases my mind and ultimately puts me at peace.

But as peaceful as this place is, I just can't seem to shut my mind off. Which I guess is understandable considering I'm pregnant with a cheater's baby.

Sighing, I throw my head back. I told myself I wasn't going to think about him. Well, that's not entirely true. I came out here to think through everything. Unfortunately, Jessie seems to dominate my thoughts.

I listen to the sounds of the crickets chirping around me and try to figure out what I'm going to do. I'm going to be raising a baby by myself. It didn't take me long to decide I was going to keep it. As much as I don't think I'm ready to be a mom, I know I could never follow through with the other thing. Of course, there's always adoption, but I don't know that I could go through with that either.

That leaves one option: keep the baby and raise it. Then, try to be a good mom while still running a business. I have no idea how I'm going to do either of those things, but damnit, I'm going to try.

I've done everything else in my life on my own—why not this?

Deciding I'm getting hungry, I pull the fish I caught this morning out of the cooler and pull out my knife to start skinning and boning it. My mind flashes back to when I was showing Jessie how to do this in my kitchen. He was so sweet to help.

*Stop it. He's an asshole. It was all an act. He was only helping to grovel for making you mad.*

Immediately, my mind flashes to the blonde standing in his living room. The blonde with giant boobs and the rocking body. The blonde who wears cute lingerie and waits for her man to get home. I'm not exactly the type.

My stomach churns as I think about what they could be doing right now. Is he bending her over and pounding into her? Is his fist wrapped around that blonde hair while she sucks him off? Is his head buried between her legs as she screams his name?

I wonder if he's going to knock her up too.

The thought of all of it makes me want to vomit. How could I have been so stupid?

All of that talk of me being a reason for him to get his life back on track? All bullshit. Every word.

And if he's capable of cheating, does that mean that he's still on the drugs? I mean, Gabby was the one he was doing it with for all that time. Are they still getting high together?

My fists clench together as I try to shove down all of the bad thoughts. It's not working, but my mind is pulled away when I hear a stick crack behind me.

Grabbing the shotgun next to me, I stand up and turn around in one swift move. When my body is facing the opposite direction, the gun's barrel is pointed right in the face of Andi.

"Whoa there, Tex! It's just me!" Her hands fly up in the air.

Quickly, I put the gun down. Hand on my hip, I ask, "What are you doing here?"

"What do you think I'm doing here? I came out here looking for you," she says, swatting a bug flying around her head.

"How'd you find me?"

Her shoulders shrug. "I went over to talk to your dad… multiple times. I figured there was no way you'd leave without telling him where to find you. I bugged him for long enough that he finally gave in and drew me a map on how to find you."

"Traitor," I mumble under my breath.

"What's with the gun?"

"I'm in the middle of the woods. What if a bear comes?"

She laughs. "You sure you're not just having target practice?" She nods over at a couple of the empty cans, which I may have taken a few angry shots at when I got here.

"Maybe. Don't come at me. I was pissed. Still am, as a matter of fact, so why don't you tell me why you're here?"

"We need to talk," she says, taking a seat on a small log.

"About?" I sit down in the lawn chair.

"About what happened yesterday."

Shaking my head, I respond, "There's nothing to talk about. I let my guard down, and I got duped. That's all there is to it."

"No, that's not all there is to it. There's actually a lot more to it that came to light after you left."

I sigh. "Andi, I don't think I want to hear any more. I don't think I can take it."

She points her finger right in my face. "Look here, Missy, I just walked through the freaking woods to come find you. You know how much I hate the woods, so you're going to listen to what I have to say."

I roll my eyes but don't argue.

She starts with, "When I got your text yesterday, I went over to see Jessie and kick the shit out of him."

"Did you see his mistress? Or am I the mistress?"

"Neither. He kicked her out."

"Super. Does he want a medal?" I ask in my most sarcastic voice.

"Damnit, Tracy, listen to me! Jessie was working late last night at the ranch. He didn't get home until after you already came over. He had no idea that Gabby was there, and the second he found out, he told her to get the hell out."

Not wanting to believe it, I shake my head. "If that's true, how did she get into the house? How did she even know where to find him?"

"Tracy, this is a small town, and although I haven't lived here all that long, here are a couple of things I've learned—things that you probably already know. One, no one here locks their doors. And two, everyone loves to talk. Gabby could have asked anyone she came upon in the street, and they would have told her exactly where to find him. It would have been even easier if she knew that he was working on the ranch. There are signs all over town leading to Mitchell Ranch."

I try to process everything she's saying to me. When I don't say anything, she lays her hand on my knee.

"Tracy, I know what you saw looked bad. I would have jumped to the same conclusion, but Jessie is a good man. And he loves you. He looked all around town for you, and now, he's just sitting in your driveway waiting on you to come home."

I don't know why my first question is, "How is he peeing if he's just sitting in his car outside my house?"

She laughs. "Trace, I don't ask questions I don't really want the answer to, but take it from someone who now has sons... they will pee *anywhere*."

"I just don't get it. Why would Gabby just show up out of the blue?"

"She's crazy. In fact, I hear she's still staying in the motel in town in hopes that Jessie changes his mind."

Okay, what the fuck is wrong with this broad? She shows up at Jessie's house and gets half-naked, and then she pines for him at the local motel? Is she really that twisted?

The pit that has been in my stomach for days is turning into white-hot rage. In one fell swoop, this chick almost destroyed everything good that we had going.

And I was about to let her. Tears burn my eyes, and Andi asks what's wrong.

"I let my insecurities and trust issues almost ruin everything," I say. "I chose to believe a woman I don't even know over a man I claim to love."

"Hey, I *know* you love him. But you're pregnant. I'm sure your emotions are running way higher than usual."

I cringe slightly at the word pregnant. That whole thing still doesn't seem real to me.

"Can we get out of here?" She asks. "I think there's some stuff you need to take care of, and I'm getting eaten alive by mosquitos. How are you not itching like crazy?"

Reaching into my bag, I pull out a can of bug spray and hold it up.

"Ah." She nods.

"I don't know that I'm ready to see or talk to him yet," I say.

"That's fine. At least you will be home and one step closer to doing it."

I start packing up my stuff. "You can go ahead and get out of here if you want. I will start making my way home."

"I'm going to have to hitch a ride with you. Jonas dropped me off here since I didn't know where I was going—even with your dad's map."

"Such a city-slicker," I laugh.

Once all of my stuff is packed up, we make our way back to my Jeep. We throw everything in the back, but I keep ahold of the shotgun, handing it to Andi as we get in.

"Hold this," I say. "We need to make a quick stop on the way."

# Chapter Forty-seven

## TRACY

Twenty minutes later, we are pulling up outside the Grady Motel. I throw the Jeep in park and get out.

"What are you doing?" Andi asks. As I grab the gun from her, she adds, "Why are you taking that?"

"You can stay here if you want. I'll only be a minute," I say.

"Not a chance in hell!" She hurries up and follows behind me.

The Grady motel is small. By small, I mean there are only eight rooms. And with only one car in the parking lot at the moment besides my own, I'm guessing only one of them is occupied.

Time to figure out which one.

I stop at the first door I come to and knock. I wait about a minute, and after hearing no noise, I move onto the next one.

"What are you going to do to her?" Andi whispers.

"I'm going to make sure she gets the message to leave Jessie alone."

"What does that mean?" She asks frantically.

There's no answer at the following three doors. Then, on door number four, I hear music on the other side. The same music I heard at Jessie's house.

Gabby has awful taste in music.

I knock on the door but make sure to keep out of view of

the peephole. When she opens the door, I push against it as hard as I can, knocking her back a couple of steps while I come inside.

"Hi. Remember me?" I ask.

She opens her mouth to speak, but I don't give her a chance.

"Let me remind you. I am not Jessie's *friend.* I'm his girlfriend. I'm the girl he's been fucking for the past month, and I'm the girl who's going to kick your ass if you don't leave us alone."

She chews on the inside of her cheek while looking me up and down as though she doesn't believe me. "What on Earth does he see in a girl like you?"

"I don't know, but it's sure as hell a lot more than he saw in you."

That hits a nerve, and she starts getting pissed. "You have no idea what Jessie and I have."

"*Had,* sweetheart. What you two *had.* You and he are finished."

"Good luck getting rid of me. I'll just keep coming back until Jessie realizes we belong together."

Andi speaks up. "That's really not a good idea."

Gabby crosses her arms over her chest. "And what are you going to do to stop me?"

Without thinking, I pull my fist back and lunge toward her as hard as I can. My knuckles make direct contact with her nose. Immediately, pain radiates through my hand, but the way Gabby's nose starts bleeding, I imagine she's in more pain than me.

"Told you that wasn't a good idea," Andi says.

"Bitch!" Gabby cries. "I'm going to call the police."

Something catches my eye on the dresser, and I walk over to it. It's a small silver tray with three lines of fine white powder on it. Cocaine.

"Go ahead," I reply. "The second they show up, I'll show them your little mess over here. Everyone here in Grady takes drug use pretty seriously. So, who do you think they're going to side with—the girl who has lived here all her life and is a respected member of the community or a junkie whore who just stumbled into town?"

She turns her head and spits out a mouth full of blood onto the red carpet.

I add. "Guess you didn't give up the lifestyle you said you did, huh?"

"No one ever really gives it up, sweetie. Even Jessie. Eventually, he will relapse. Everyone does."

I shake my head. "I'm done believing everyone else besides him."

"That's on you. You'll feel stupid when you see him falling back into his old ways. Jessie told me about how his father was— always stepping back into the lifestyle. Do you know how many times Jessie told me he was going to quit and then went right back to it?"

"There's a difference now. He has me, and I won't encourage that kind of behavior like you did."

"We'll see," she says with an overabundance of confidence. "I'll be waiting when he changes his mind."

This woman has been making me more and more angry ever since we started talking, and I just can't take any more. Something in me snaps.

That crazy side that I've been trying to tamp down for years? She has risen to the service and is demanding her presence be felt.

Grabbing Gabby by the throat, I back her up against the wall, pinning her there.

"Listen here, bitch! You're not going to wait for him. You are going to get in your car and take your happy little ass back to Nashville."

She struggles to take a deep breath and says, "And what if I don't?"

I hold up the shotgun in my left hand. "You said it yourself. I'm fucking crazy. Do you really want to find out?"

For the first time, I see something in her eyes other than pure confidence—fear.

With that, I let her go and turn towards the door, gesturing Andi to follow me. Her eyes are as wide as saucers as she closes the door behind us.

"You *are* a little crazy. Do you know that?" She whispers as we walk toward the Jeep.

I shrug. "I know. I actually used to be a lot worse."

Her eyes go wide again. "After that little incident, I find that hard to believe."

# Chapter Forty-eight

## JESSIE

I've lost count of how many hours I've been sitting in Tracy's driveway. Every hour that passes, I feel a little more hopeless.

Andi said she would talk to Tracy's dad, but she texted me saying she hadn't gotten very far. She told me she'd call if she figured anything out, but I haven't heard another word.

I pray to God that Tracy will listen to me when I finally do see her again. And I pray to God that she believes what I have to say.

When the driver's seat of my truck gets uncomfortable, I walk around for a few minutes before hopping up into the bed. I'm here for the long haul, so I'm trying to switch it up a little.

Marlow has already been out twice to ask me what I was doing. I answered her as politely as possible, telling her I was waiting on Tracy, but the way she pursed her lips, I don't think she believed me.

Whatever. I don't care about that old woman's opinion.

I only care about one person's opinion right now. And she doesn't want to talk to me.

My phone rings in my pocket, and I jump to answer it. I don't even look at the screen before clicking the green ON button.

"Hello?"

Jonas's voice comes through the other end. "Hey man, just checking in. How'd everything go?"

"What are you talking about? I'm still sitting in Tracy's driveway."

"Oh," he says with a long pause.

"What's going on?"

He sighs as if he just told me something he wasn't supposed to. "Andi tracked down Tracy. I dropped her off a couple of hours ago. I figured they made their way back to you by now."

"She found her?! Where?"

"I don't know details, man." I sense he's lying, but I have a feeling I've just asked him to reveal something his wife told him in confidence, so I don't press.

"Well, if it was a couple of hours ago, I'm guessing it's not going well. Maybe she wouldn't listen to Andi."

"Don't underestimate my wife's powers of persuasion. If anyone can talk Tracy off a ledge, it's Andi. Don't worry. I'm sure they'll be there soon." He tries to be reassuring, but none of it is helping.

"Just call me if you hear from either of them, okay?" I ask.

He agrees, and we hang up. I wonder where Tracy's been hiding. If Andi found her, it probably wasn't very far. But if they weren't very far, why aren't they back here yet?

My stomach twists, wondering what she's going to say to me when I finally do see her. Is she going to tell me to fuck off? I probably would. Even if she believes me, I won't blame her if she thinks I have way too much baggage—that my past is too much for her.

But I at least have to try—even if it doesn't have a happy ending.

I debate starting up the truck and driving around looking for her, but I don't want to take the chance of missing her when she gets back.

My hands rub my eyes, trying to stay awake. I have no idea how long I've been up for now, and even though the cold medicine has made me feel better, it's drained me of every scrap of energy.

My eyelids grow heavy as I feel myself slowly losing the battle. But when I hear a car pull up behind my truck, I get my second wind.

But when I glance in the rearview mirror, it's not at all who I want it to be. Instead of Tracy's car, I see one of the town cop cars.

*Fuck me.*

I step out of my truck and walk toward Officer Graves. This old son-of-a-bitch has never liked me. Of course, it might have something to do with the fact that he once caught me smoking weed with his son in their barn.

That didn't go over well. I'm surprised he didn't throw a party when I left town since I was such a 'bad influence' on his son.

"Officer Graves," I greet.

"Mr. Mitchell," he says, pulling his pants up by his large belt. "Care to tell me what you're doing here?"

"Waiting on someone."

He looks around. "Boy, you can't just hang out in someone's driveway for days on end. You're freaking out the neighbors."

My eyes roll back. "Let me guess. Marlow called you."

"Boy, it's not important who called me." He pulls a toothpick out of his pocket and sticks it between his teeth. "You look like you're up to no good around here. You planning on robbing this house or something?"

I'm getting really sick of this guy calling me 'boy.' "No, I told you I'm waiting for someone. And I'm not leaving. She should be back anytime."

"Boy, if you aren't going to leave on your own, you can explain it to the judge." He pulls out a set of handcuffs off the holder on his belt.

I could run or struggle against him, but I know it's pointless. Instead, I try to talk my way out of it. After all, I won't see Tracy for who knows how long if I'm sitting in jail.

I decide to tell him I'm sorry and I'll get out of here, but before I can even open my mouth, I hear a different voice behind me.

"Officer Graves, what's going on here?"

*Tracy.*

The officer turns his head. "Miss Kennedy. We got a report from your neighbor that this gentleman was loitering on your property. Seemed pretty suspicious, so I was going to take him in for questioning."

"Officer, please let him go. I asked Jessie to wait here for me, and due to some personal business, I got held up a little longer than expected. He's done nothing wrong."

Despite Tracy getting into some trouble off and on when we were younger, everyone in this town loves her—even the cops.

Officer Graves sighs and releases my hands. "You got off lucky this time, boy." Then, leaning in to whisper, he adds, "Better watch your back."

Then, he turns and gets back into his car, and drives off.

I look at Tracy. Despite the solemn look on her face, she still looks beautiful.

"Thank you," I say. "Old bastard has been waiting for a chance to nail me for years."

"You're welcome," she mumbles, her green eyes staring into mine.

Andi steps out of her Jeep and walks up behind her, but I don't care that she's there. I will say what I need to say no matter who is listening.

But before I can say a word, Tracy cuts me off, "I know we need to talk, but I'm exhausted, and I need a shower. And considering you've been living in my driveway, I think you could use one too. I'll text you later, and we will meet up. For now, do you think you could give Andi a ride home?"

I want to argue and tell her that we need to talk *now,* but that isn't going to help matters. Tracy heads toward her house and walks inside without another word.

My eyes look over at Andi, who is giving me a weak smile. She says, "Don't worry. She'll come around. She's had a big day."

I open the passenger door of the truck for her, and she slides on in. When I get in and close my door, I say, "Is there anything that you can tell me without breaking some sort of 'best friend code'?"

"Well, I told her about the whole misunderstanding, and she admits maybe she freaked out a little more than she should."

My head shakes back and forth as I keep my eyes fixed on the road in front of me. "I don't blame her. I'd have a whole hell of a lot of questions if a half-naked man were answering her door."

"It was just a bad situation all around. But the bright side is that I don't think Gabby will be bothering you anymore."

"What do you mean?"

Her mouth twists around as though she's searching for exactly how to tell me. "Let's just say Tracy scared her half to death."

"Say more," I command.

She sighs and pushes one of her dark curls out of her eyes. "I told Tracy Gabby was still staying at the motel, so she went to talk to her. When Gabby wasn't exactly getting the message, Tracy sort of…punched her and pretty much told her that if she came back, she'd shoot her."

"What?!" Now, my wide eyes look at Andi.

"Yeah…"

Out of all the reactions I could have at this moment, I have the one you'd least expect. I start laughing. Hysterically laughing.

Andi looks at me like I'm insane, but I can't help it.

I glance over at her and say, "That's the Tracy I know. Back in the day, she was a firecracker. No, scratch that. She was a fucking pistol. She grew up and calmed down a bit, but that wild heart is still inside. I'm just glad to see it hasn't faded away."

"No, I'd say her inner badass came out to say hello. She pretty much told Gabby to leave the two of you alone. Oh, and there was cocaine on the dresser, and she told her to stay away from you with all that too. Face it, Jess, Tracy will stand up for what she believes in, but you're the hill she would die on."

It gives me a warm feeling that she was willing to fight for our love—even after everything that happened.

I can't wait to talk to her and show her just how much I'm willing to fight too.

# Chapter Forty-nine

## TRACY

It's been close to six hours since I've been home, and after a good nap and now sitting in a warm bubble bath, I feel like I'm starting to feel a bit more like myself.

I don't know if it's the stress of everything or the tiny human sharing my body, but I have just felt *off.*

Reaching forward, I add some more hot water to the tub and lean back as it fills. I can't remember the last time I slowed down long enough to take a bubble bath. Typically, a shower just seems faster—not to mention more sanitary. After all, isn't a bath sort of like just sitting in your own filth?

I try not to think about that, though, and just think about the relaxing aspect.

Once the water is once again warm enough to my liking, I turn the water off and lean back once more. My fingers splash in the water as I pop a couple of tiny bubbles.

My eyes glance down at my stomach. On the outside, there is no sign that there's a baby in there yet. But I guess the little guy or gal has set up shop in my uterus.

I begin talking out loud as though the baby is going to hear me. Maybe it can. I have no idea.

"Okay, you…listen up. So far, you have made your mother an emotional mess, and let me tell you, emotions are not really my thing—except anger. I seem to be pretty good at that one. But since you came on the scene, I seem to be a little all over the map. So, how about I'll make you a deal. You take it easy on me these next nine months, and I'll try to take it easy on you when you get here."

My hand lays on my stomach, where I assume the tiny peanut is positioned. "I have a feeling your daddy is going to be way better at this whole parenthood thing than I am. He is quite a bit more affectionate than I am at times—and far more patient. But, despite those things, I haven't given him many benefits of the doubt that past few days. In fact, I thought the absolute worst of him.

"I haven't told him about you yet, but I know when I do, he's going to be so happy."

*At least I hope he will be so happy.*

"I should probably go talk to him, huh? I guess we can't stay in the bathtub forever. We will get all pruny."

Despite not being thrilled about this pregnancy, talking to my unborn baby makes me feel cathartic—as though I'm getting some sort of clarity I didn't have before.

Maybe that whole pregnancy brain is starting to kick in, and I'm just losing my mind. But maybe there's something to the whole mother-baby bond thing.

I sit in the tub for just a little longer until the water cools off yet again, and then I wrap myself in a towel and step out. Once I am out and dry, I find my phone and type out a message to Jessie.

**Meet me at our spot in an hour?**

## Chapter Fifty

JESSIE

*T* *hank God.*

That's the thought that has run through my head ever since Tracy texted me a little while ago. And let me say, it's been a long-ass hour waiting for her. I practically sprinted to the secluded lake, and I've been waiting for her, hoping she might get here a little early.

Part of me is bracing for her to tell me to fuck off—that I'm too much of a damaged soul for her to bother with. I pray that's not what happens, but I'm preparing for the worst. Better to be surprised with good news than disappointed with bad.

I keep pulling my phone out of my pocket, but I immediately put it back the second I unlock it. I guess I'm just fidgeting.

After what feels like an eternity has passed, I hear some footsteps coming up the path. When my eyes glance up, I see Tracy emerging from the clearing in the trees.

She looks beautiful—somehow more beautiful than ever before. Her wavy hair slightly moves in the wind, and the sunlight highlights her freckles. She's wearing a tye-dye tank top and a pair of white jean shorts, which show off her tan.

She walks toward me but doesn't make direct eye contact, instead looking at the ground where she's stepping. When she reaches me, our eyes finally meet, but I can't read anything within hers.

"Hi," she says before taking a seat next to me.

"Hey, baby girl." I pause for a moment to see if she's going to yell at me for calling her that, but she doesn't.

"T, I am so sorry," I begin without giving her time to change her mind and run in the opposite direction.

"Jessie, you don't have to—"

"Yes, I do. Look, when I went to Nashville, I thought I had gotten Gabby out of my life. I had no idea she would show up in my house half-naked and believe me when I say I was pissed about it. I told her to get the fuck out, and I was done. I told her I was in love with you, and nothing was going to change that. When she left, I was planning on coming to tell you right away, but then, Andi showed up and said you were gone, and things just snowballed." I'm rambling now, and I've barely come up for air.

I slow down and try to be calmer. "Sorry, the speech I had coming in here was much better than the one I'm giving now. T, you and I have had something so special the past month. Hell, we've had something special our whole lives—since the day I met you. How many people can you say met their soulmate when they were five years old? That doesn't happen every day, and if I gave you any type of impression that I am not one hundred percent devoted to you, I am so sorry."

She reaches up and puts one finger over my lips to silence me. It doesn't work, though, because I keep talking; now, it's just a bit more muffled.

"I love you so fucking much, T. I will do anything I can to show that to you. I'm sorry I'm so messed up, but I promise I'm trying to do better."

Now, she grabs me by the shirt collar and pulls me in, pressing her lips to mine. It's not a long kiss, and when she pulls back, she says, "Will you shut up for a minute?"

"Yes, ma'am."

She smiles. "Don't call me ma'am. Don't get me wrong— what happened was awful, and I hope never to have to see that ever again." She paused for a moment. "But I should have given you the benefit of the doubt. I shouldn't have jumped to the worst possible conclusion, and I normally wouldn't have. I just… haven't been feeling like myself lately."

"You have nothing to be sorry for, T. I should have made it more clear to Gabby that the door for us was closed and would never be open again."

She stops me once again. "Hey, wild child, I just apologized to you. Accept it. Dating me, it probably won't happen very often."

"So, we are still dating?" I ask timidly.

Her lips curl up into a wide smile. "Yes, we are still dating. I'm not going to let that stupid bitch ruin what you and I have. And I'm sorry for leaving that in question."

Without thinking another second, I pull her close to me. My lips practically attack hers. One hand buries in her hair while the other holds the small of her back, pulling her even closer. My tongue runs along the seam of her lips, begging for entrance. She readily grants it, and I delve inside.

Her fingers fist in my hair, and she releases a little moan into my mouth. There is only one way to describe how it feels having her back in my arms.

Home.

Every worry or doubt I've had the past two days melts away as if they never existed.

Gently, I lean her back so that she's now lying on the deck. Our kiss intensifies, but before it can go any further, I feel her hand on my chest, pushing me away.

Our lip lock breaks and she looks at me. "As good as this is, I need to tell you something before we keep going."

"Anything."

"I'm pregnant."

## Chapter Fifty-one

### TRACY

The words come out of my mouth, and I have no idea how Jessie will react. He's quiet for a moment as if trying to process the information I just laid on him. I don't blame him—it's a pretty big bomb I just dropped.

But it doesn't take long before a big smile breaks out on his face. "Pregnant? Are you sure?"

"Well, I haven't been to the doctor yet, but believe me when I say that there was no denying that POSITIVE on the test."

He grabs my face and kisses me. When he pulls back, he has tears in his eyes.

"Hey, what's wrong?" I ask.

His hands hold mine. "Not a damn thing. I'm so fucking happy, T." One of those hands goes to lay on my belly. "You're carrying our baby."

I nod, trying to look as enthusiastic as he is.

He notices my unease, though. "Hey, baby girl, talk to me. What's going on? Tell me what you're thinking."

As I begin to speak, my voice cracks, signaling the outpouring of emotions I'm about to have. "I just...things were going so well. I don't want anything to change that."

"T, I'm not going to tell you things aren't going to change. They are," he says while I try to stifle a sniffle.

He continues, "But they're not going to change for the bad.

I'm not going to let them. Things will change because we are going to have a new little person to take care of. That doesn't mean everything has to change, though."

Now, the tears are streaming freely. I hate being this emotional. "What about my job?"

"What about it?"

Through my tiny sobs, I manage to get out, "I…can't…be… a…mom…and…run…a…business."

His forehead creases. "Who the hell told you that?"

"I mean, everyone in this town gets pregnant, and then that's it. They give up everything else."

He cuts me off. "And I don't know if that's just a small-town mentality or what, but once you get out of Grady, it's not like that. T, in Nashville, you saw women everywhere who had it all—a family and a career. The two don't have to be mutually exclusive."

"Were those women letting nannies raise their kids?"

He shrugs. "Sometimes, yes. Sometimes, no. Tracy, I'm never going to tell you not to work. You love your job, and I am so proud of you for everything you've accomplished. Hell, I'll stay home with the baby if it'll make you happy."

I let out a small chuckle. "You're going to stay home while I bring home the bacon? Isn't that some major blow to your male ego?"

"Baby girl, I could care less about my male ego. Most men see taking care of their women as bringing home the money and leaving it at that. Everything else still falls on the women's shoulders. If I can take care of you by staying home with our baby and keeping on everything else so you don't have to, I'm okay with that."

I bury my head in my hands. "How do you always know the perfect things to say?"

"I don't. But I know I love you, and I know that we are going to have the cutest baby in the whole wild world."

When I look up at him again, he's smiling, showing off those beautiful pearly whites.

"Yeah, it'll probably be pretty cute, huh?"

"The cutest!" He exclaims.

We both laugh for a minute, and Jessie wipes away the tears.

"I'm warning you now," I begin. "I'm an emotional mess. I cry over everything like a little bitch. And I'm tired all the time, and for once, I'm not that hungry because this baby is making me nauseous all the time."

"I don't care about the crying. And we can nap together when you're tired. As for not being hungry? I'm sure that will pass."

"And I'll get fat."

He smiles. "Pregnant—not fat. And I'll love you no matter what you look like. I'll still get you naked and take advantage of you."

"You better," I mutter.

He pulls me close to him and holds me as we sit in comfortable silence for a little while. I look around at the lake, taking it all in. This place has meant so much to us over the years, and it seemed only fitting that I give him the biggest news of our lives here.

My head leans against Jessie's chest, and I feel my eyes getting heavy as I listen to the sound of his rhythmic heartbeat. With him stroking my hair, it honestly seems like a perfect moment.

I have no idea how long we've been here when Jessie starts to pull away.

He takes a deep breath before speaking as though he's nervous about something.

"What's wrong, sweets?" I ask.

"Nothing. I just...I need you to know that I'm not doing this because of the baby. I've been planning this for a while—you can ask Andi. I've just been waiting for the right time to do it, and right now...here...it seems right."

I have no idea what he's talking about until he pulls a ring out of his pocket.

Oh no…here come the waterworks again.

He holds up the ring. "I had a whole speech planned, but at this moment, I remember none of it, so I'm just going to wing it."

Apparently, the cat's got my tongue, and all I can do is nod.

"Tracy Kennedy, I think I knew you were the girl for me the first day I met you. When you punched that kid in the nose for me, I knew you'd always have my back. And you have…even when maybe I didn't have yours. I'm so sorry it took me so long to get my head out of my ass, but I promise I'm never letting you go ever again. I know without a doubt that I don't deserve you, but that won't stop me from trying to make you happy."

"You do make me happy," I interject.

"Good." He smiles. "And I promise I'm not asking you this because you're pregnant. I wanted to marry you long before that. And maybe we haven't been back together for all that long, but as I said, I've wanted to marry you for a long time. So, I'm finally asking the question. Will you marry me?"

"Yes!" Before I can finish getting the word out, he pulls me into his arms, hugging me so tight, I can barely breathe.

"Jess, the baby and I still need oxygen," I whisper.

"Sorry," he says, pulling back. "Just excited."

He slips the ring on my finger. It's not huge, which I appreciate because I am not a huge jewelry fan. The smaller, the better.

My arms snake around his neck and pull him close to me. My lips touch his, lightly at first and then with more fire and passion. It doesn't take long before both of us are enthralled and breathless.

My hand reaches between us, and I feel the hard bulge in his jeans. When I give it a gentle squeeze, he breaks the kiss.

"Baby girl, as tempted as I am to fuck you right here on this dock, I don't want someone to walk up on us randomly. Besides, the things I want to do to you require a big, comfortable bed. Let's go back to your place."

I nod, but as we stand up, I say, "Your place is closer."

# Chapter Fifty-two

## JESSIE

Tracy is pregnant with my baby. And she agreed to marry me. This must be what utter, and complete happiness feels like.

The moment we get back to my place, I swoop her up in my arms and carry her up the porch steps and inside.

When we walk right in, Tracy giggles. "When are you going to learn to start locking your doors?"

"I should probably start, huh?" I ask, carrying her straight to the bedroom.

The moment we are there, I lay her down as gently as possible and begin to kiss her. Each time our lips meet, I can feel the love we have for each other. And I'm going to spend all night showing her just how much she means to me.

My fingertips roam all over her body while our tongues dance. The way she's angling her hips toward me lets me know she's anxious, but I'm going to take my time and savor every second—every touch—every taste.

My kisses shift from her mouth to her neck and the top of her chest. She lets out a moan every time I use my teeth to nip at the soft flesh.

I can see her nipples getting hard through her shirt, so I take a moment to nip at those through the thin fabric as well gently. She arches her back, forcing her chest closer to me. It pleads for more attention.

"You want me to play with these, baby?" My fingers prick at one of the stiff peaks.

"Mmm-hmm," she whines.

Determined to give her what she wants, I tug her shirt off over her head and use my mouth to trail kisses all around her breasts but never quite making contact where she craves it the most.

When my tongue finally flicks over the sensitive bud, she shudders beneath me. Her hands fist in my hair as I alternate between licking and sucking.

I can tell that she's getting wet by the way she's writhing beneath me. Slowly, I move down further, making sure to plant kisses all over her stomach in the process.

I tease her by taking my time, pulling her shorts and panties down her legs and off her body. Once they're off, I start at her right ankle, kissing all the way up her calf, her knee, and then her thigh. Finally, I stop just short of her pretty pussy and do the same thing on the other leg.

When I am done, she's panting. "Damnit, Jessie! Touch me!"

I spread apart her lips, showing just how wet she is for me and giving me perfect access to her clit. My thumb reaches out to rub it, light, slow circles at first and then increasing pressure as I go.

Her hands cover her face as her legs begin to shake.

"Let me see it, baby girl," I tell her.

Her hands move from her face to grip the sheets around her. She's close; I can tell by how much her legs are quivering.

"Oh God, Jessie! I'm going to..." she cries, unable to even finish her sentence.

When she's about to fall over the edge, I replace my fingers with my mouth, sucking on her clit while my tongue flicks up and down against it.

Her body explodes with her orgasm. Waves of pleasure wash over her time and time again as I wring every drop of it from her body.

When she stills, my finger rubs the soft flesh once again, and she practically bucks off the bed from the sensitivity.

Tracy grabs me and pulls me close, kissing me and tasting herself on my mouth.

When she leans back, there's a hunger in her eyes, and she whispers two words that make my impossibly hard dick even harder.

"My turn."

## Chapter Fifty-three

TRACY

Holy shit. That might have been the biggest orgasm I've ever had. I don't know how that man does these things to my body, but man, I love that he does them.

Wasting no time, I practically rip his clothes from his body before crawling between his legs.

I'm on my knees with my ass up in the air as I take his cock in my mouth, swirling my tongue around the head. I tease him by taking a long slow lick from the base all the way to the head and back down again.

When I move a little further down and focus on his balls, he lets out a low growl. And when I go back to his dick and take it down my throat, his hand holds my hair back but never pulls or forces me to take more than I'm comfortable with.

I bob up and down on him, my hand joining in to stroke him at the same time.

"Fuck, baby girl," he moans.

When I speed up my tempo, he uses his grip on my hair to pull me off of him. "T, as much as I would love to come in your mouth, I need to fuck you."

We both sit up, and he positions me how he wants me. First, he lays me on my side with one of my legs propped up on his shoulder. Then, he gets on his knees and slides into me. We fit together perfectly—like two puzzle pieces that have always belonged together.

From this angle, he can get impossibly deep as he glides in with long, smooth strokes. One of his large hands holds my legs in place while using the other to hold onto my hip.

Every time he pushes in, I feel him making contact with my already-sensitive clit. If he keeps this up, I'll be coming again in no time.

He looks down at me, and his eyes not only show his hunger for me, but they show his love. There's no mistaking the connection that Jessie and I share.

I see the sweat starting to break out on his forehead, and I know he's getting close but trying to hold out to get me off again.

"Harder," I plead. "Fuck me harder."

He does as I ask and pounds into me with more enthusiasm. It doesn't take long before both of us are crying out while we come.

When he pulls out of me, he goes to the bathroom to get a rag to clean us both up. After he's done, he lies down next to me and pulls me close, wrapping his arm around me.

"Do you know how much I love you?" He whispers against the back of my neck.

"I think I've got a pretty good idea, but you can tell me anyway," I joke.

I feel his body shake with laughter. Then, when he stills, he says, "Tracy Kennedy, I promise you that I will do anything in the world for you. You make me endlessly happy."

I decide to make him even happier. "You know pretty soon, you'll have to stop calling me Tracy Kennedy. I'll have a new last time."

His head pokes up, and he turns me to look at him. "You want to take my last name?"

I shrug. "I figure our baby will have your last name. I don't want to be left out."

Grabbing my face, he pulls me in for another kiss. "Well, okay then, Mrs. Mitchell. But I think we need to talk about how maybe it's time to stop punching people…"

# Chapter Fifty-four

## JESSIE

"Jessie. Jessie, wake up, sweets." Tracy is whispering in my ear and trying to shake me awake.

"Hmmm?" I grumble.

"Get up. There's something I want to show you. You don't want to miss it. Come on. I'll drive."

"We're leaving the house?"

She tugs on my arm but doesn't make much progress.

Leaning in, she whispers, "When we get done, I'll take all my clothes off."

That's enough to make me sit straight up and get dressed. Tracy is already dressed and ready to go. She even hands me a to-go cup of coffee before we head out the door.

We jump in her Jeep, and she drives rather quickly on the way to her house.

Once we are there, she practically sprints out of the Jeep and up to her porch but doesn't go inside. Instead, she has a seat on one of the chairs she has sitting there.

"Have a seat." She gestures to the empty chair beside her.

Once I sit down, she says, "And now we wait."

"What are we waiting for?" I ask.

She takes a sip of her coffee and replies, "You'll see."

A few minutes later, we see a car pulling onto the road and headed this way.

I watch the red sedan heading toward us when Tracy says, "Remember me telling you that Marlow has a side piece? A younger guy she has come over after her husband goes to work at three AM?"

"Yeah..."

"Well, this morning, I called Marlow's husband and told him I heard some booming noises coming from their house, and he might want to come home to check it out before I call the police. He assured me he was going to come home to check it out."

Right as she finishes speaking, a car zooms into the driveway across the street and comes to a screeching halt.

I haven't seen much of Marlow's husband, but he's a tall, husky man who only has to take a few long strides to get into the house. It's a matter of moments before we hear some crashing around in the house, and then the screen door slams open once more.

A much younger man in his boxers comes running out of the house with Marlow's husband right behind him.

"You think you can just fuck my wife and get away with it, boy?!" The burly man yells.

The kid takes off running around the house, and the man chases after him. They run a couple of laps, and it's hysterical—almost like something you'd see in a cartoon.

Marlow runs out in a very small robe and joins in the fight. "Tom! Tom, leave him alone!"

"Stay out of this Marlow!" He points at his wife. "You and I will talk about this once I teach this boy a lesson."

Marlow stomps her foot and throws her hands on her hips, watching the scene in front of her. She pleads with her husband to let it go and yells at him that it's his own damn fault for not giving her any attention.

I look over, and Tracy is cracking up, admiring her handiwork.

Apparently, Marlow notices too because she looks over and crosses her arms in front of her chest.

Tracy holds up her hand and waves, still laughing her ass

off.

When Tom finally gets tired and stops chasing the boy, he walks over to Marlow. "What the hell is wrong with you?" He asks before stepping inside.

Tracy turns toward me. "Payback is a bitch. That's what she gets for trying to have you arrested yesterday." She smiles before adding, "Come on, let's head inside."

I follow her into the house, and she sets her mug down on the counter. I spin her around so she's facing me.

"You're a little crazy, T. Do you know that?" I ask, pulling her close to me.

She holds up her finger and thumb an inch apart. "Maybe just a little. And let me just say that this baby is already bringing out my inner crazy."

"So, maybe you will be going back to being the wild child for the next nine months?"

She smiles. "Probably. But I think with parents like us, this baby will be the true wild child."

I get on my knees in front of her and start talking to her belly. "Listen here, baby. You better take it easy on your momma. Between you and her, that's an awful lot of crazy."

She playfully punches my shoulder. My eyes look up at her and back to her belly, and I can't believe in the course of a month, I have gotten everything I've ever wanted—or should I say, everything I never knew I always wanted.

When Tracy walked back into my life, I knew she would be my reason to stay clean. My reason to continue to live a life in a town where I felt utterly alone. My reason to wake up every day and try to be a better person.

And now, our baby will add to that list of reasons.

Our little wild child.

## Chapter Fifty-five

### TRACY

*One year later...*

"Baby, I'm home!" I call as I walk through the front door of our new home. Well, *newer,* I guess. We've lived here for about six months now.

After we drew up some plans, Jessie's brother, Jared, built it for us. It's not huge, but it's plenty of space for us—and it even has a little extra if we ever grow our family by one more. Not that either of us is in any hurry to make that happen.

I take off my jacket and head into the living room. Still not finding Jessie, I walk toward our bedroom. When I get there, I find Jessie asleep, holding our beautiful baby girl on his chest.

Leaning against the doorway, I cross my arms and take a moment to just gaze at them. Four months ago, little Nora came into our lives. She was almost an entire month early, and when I went into labor, I barely made it through the hospital doors before she made her grand entrance. She came into this world on her terms, and she's been just as headstrong ever since.

I may have carried her for all that time, but she looks just like Jessie with a head full of dark hair and crystal blue eyes. But her attitude (and her appetite) are all mine.

I thought being pregnant would be awful, but the first time I felt little Nora kick inside my belly, everything just sort of clicked. And the first time I laid eyes on her? My world shifted yet again. Nora and I may be Jessie's reasons for staying clean and sober, but the two of them are also my reason for everything I do now.

Jessie and I did get married, but we waited until Nora was born and had her be part of the small ceremony. She will in no way remember any of it, but I loved having her there on our special day.

I still work and run the business, but I try to find a nice balance between work and home. I don't want to miss my baby growing up if I'm always working. Jamie has stepped up and helped me out a ton around the store, so I offered her some equity in the business. She happily accepted and has transitioned into her new role flawlessly.

Jessie still works at the ranch a couple of days a week while his mom watches Nora. We don't necessarily need the money, but he enjoys getting out of the house, and I think Jonas appreciates the help.

Speaking of Jonas, he and Andi were finally able to adopt Kyle and Keith, so their little family is finally official—in the eyes of the government, that is. They've always been official to us.

Jessie shifts on the bed and opens his eyes. I guess he could feel me staring at him.

"Hey, beautiful. When did you get home?" He smiles.

"Just a minute ago."

As he begins to get up, Nora shifts and starts to wake up too. I swear she's his little twin. Their connection is something special.

"Nora, my love, look...Mommy's home!" He says as she snuggles against his chest.

When we make eye contact, she gives me an adorable toothless smile.

"Hi, beautiful!" I say, walking toward them and reaching out my arms. She reaches for me, and my heart melts.

When she's in my arms, I sniff the top of her head, inhaling the addictive baby smell.

Jessie stands up and wraps his arms around both of us.

This.

This is what happiness truly feels like. A year ago, I thought I was happy. Back then, I was. I was pleased with my life and living it by myself and on my terms. My life wasn't bad. But there was just something missing—I just had no idea of that fact.

When Jessie and I reconnected, it was like something that had been gone for so long finally showed back up. It was like the other half to my whole reappeared. And then, Nora became another piece of the puzzle we didn't know we were missing.

"Come on, girls," Jessie says. "I'll make us some dinner."

I crack a smile at how my husband can go back and forth so quickly between his dirty-mouthed sexy time and full-on dad mode. It's a fine line, but he walks it well.

As we are walking out of the bedroom, he playfully smacks my ass and whispers, "Those jeans are really working for me. So tonight, I'm going to pin your legs to the headboard and go to town."

Okay...so maybe the lines are *a little* blurred.

# *What's next in Grady?*

Fall in love with Jared and Kris in All the
Right Choices, coming Fall 2021!

Preorder your copy at https://www.amazon.com/
gp/product/B096W1ZL4K

# Books by Stephanie Renee

**<u>The Constant Series:</u>**

*A Constant Surprise*

*A Constant Reminder*

*A Constant Love*

*A Constant Christmas (a holiday novella)*

**<u>Standalone spin-offs:</u>**

*Seeing Red*

*Aces Wild*

**<u>Grady Romances:</u>**

*All the Right Things*

*All the Right Reasons*

*All the Right Choices (coming Fall 2021)*

**<u>Standalones:</u>**

*Beauty and the Boss Man (coming Summer 2021)*

# About The Author

## Stephanie Renee

Stephanie is a Mid-Western girl living in Indiana with her husband, their two sons, and their two big fur babies. She's addicted to strong coffee and cheap wine. When she isn't writing, she loves to get sucked into the newest true crime documentary while spending time with her family.